The Block Is Hot:

A Classic Hood Novel

By: JAE JEWEllZ

DEDICATION

This book is dedicated to my cousin TyShawn "Dutch" Mathews my true Buffalo Souljah. May you continue to be our guardian angel and watch over us all.

ACKNOWLEDGEMENTS

First and foremost, I would like to give all praises to the man above, without him none of this would be possible! Second I would like to thank my mother and father my grandparents and my brother Porda for their constant encouragement throughout this journey. Don't hold it against me when you do read this book, cause its some ungodly things going on LOL.

To my husband Corey I thank you for supporting me and picking up the slack when I needed you to. From the brainstorming and staying up late and listening to me reading the story to you out loud, your support means the world to me. I know it wasn't easy putting up with me during the beginning of this journey but I thank you and love you dearly for it.

To my bestie Tokoiya Williams, Yasssss Bish! I remember telling you that I wanted to write a book and you immediately went out and brought me a notebook and pens. Came back and slapped it in my lap and said let's get to writing this book bish. Lol ma nigga thanks for the push!

My Cleveland chick Kelley Lewis you would call me once a month and ask me if I picked up a pen yet. When you first said it you told me god told you to tell me to pick the pen back up. At the time we had no idea what it meant, but I thank you for being an obident child of God and relaying his words. And staying on me about it too! Thank you boo. Just know I value your friendship very much. Love ya chick.

To my Goodyear Family! Standup ma nigga we made it. Yall will forever have a special place in my heart no matter where on earth I may be GY till the death of me!!

To ma nigga P. Serentity, ma muse. Thanks for all the times we stayed up late on the phone brainstorming and reading back scenes to each other. Half the time we weren't even talking we just stayed on the phone because we gave each other the juice. Jaz playing DJ in the background so we had our music. The love and support has been real from the very beginning.

Niq you been with me since the very beginning, you were my first test reader. There had been times when I felt like giving up but you wouldn't let me and I love you so much for that.

Ash and Zaii I appreciate you chicks for the late night brainstorming sessions with me as well and staying on me about not giving up. Ash is the queen at finding sexy character pics lol. And Zaii is a hell of a proof reader.

Kana Boo you were always the voice of reason in my crazy world. I was in a very dark place during this journey and you were the light that helped me get through. I appreciate you sis! Hugs and kisses.

To the rest of my PH2016 sisters Tay, Britt brat, and Lena without all of you chicks I don't know where I would have been. Yall stayed on me about getting it done and much more. We were all like sisters from another mother, and Im lucky to have had yall in my corner. # nigga we made it.

There has been a lot of people that has supported me in the journey to becoming an author Briann Denae thank you boo for always being there when I needed a listening ear your support has always been real. Nako you schooled me on the game and encouraged me since the beginning and I appreciate you boo! It was because of you that I met some of the most amazing women ever.

My boo D'Yereka you and Laquanda have been awesome test readers and friends. D'Yereka you would hit me up every so often and ask me how far I had gotten and what happened next. At one point I wanted to give up but you wouldn't let me. It was your encouragement and your love for the story that made me believe in myself and fall back in love with the story again. Thanks chick I owe you a drink or two or four.

To Tiara and Kia my pen sisters you wanches are some of the coolest and most down to earth woman I know lol. You chicks embraced me and welcomed me in with no hesitation, and we have been rocking ever since. I love yall crazy chicks. To Kosha Jordan hunni you didn't know me from a can of paint but you supported me and rooted me on since day one, trust boo it doesn't go unnoticed. I owe you a signed copy of this book and you will be one of the first to get yours.

Now yall know this is my first book so this section is a little long, but I had to thank each and every one of you for playing a major part in this excursion so bear with me yall. I promise in the next book it will be shorter lol.

Last but not mutha fuckin least my publisher Tiece and her right hand man Ebony. I would like to thank you Queens for this great opportunity and also for believing in me enough to give me a shot at my dreams that's all I needed. You ladies are the real MVP's. Now let's continue to put out this heat. They ain't got no choice but to put RESPECK on TMP when they say it! Lol. Now let's get this skrilla ladies!!

Thank you to all who have supported me, trust it doesn't go unnoticed. Without further a due I hope you all enjoy my baby, my first creation, one of many more to come! Thanks for reading.

Find me on Facebook @ **yagirlquitadonechanged**

Like my author page as well at **Author Jae Jewellz**

Instagram and Twitter: Jae Jewellz

For group discussions, giveaways, games, for personal interaction with me and more! Join my reading group today on Facebook called: The Block

Block

"Niggas don't respect you until you become disrespectful; you feel me?" Block said, taking a long pull from his blunt of Kush, while bobbing his head to the new John Halkz track, *Get Back Home.*

"I hear what you saying B; I... I mean, I feel you," Tone stuttered while trying to gather his lies. "I'm saying though, ma dude, all I need is one more week jus... just one more we-"

"Aye, shut up nigga, this my part," Block said, then continued rapping along with his new favorite artist.

They show me love when I get back home

It's either Remy or Patron when I get back home

They ask why you been gone when I get back

I said I'm tryna put on fa the kids back home, you know

Block turned the volume all the way up. He was sitting in his all black 2015 Chevy Tahoe with 26-inch black alloy rims. The speakers in his truck was thumping and this track was knocking extra hard. Block continued to rap along with John Halkz.

They show me love when I

Pow –Pow!

Block jumped in his seat and turned around as he turned the volume down. He looked in the backseat at his best friend Leno like, "What the fuck you shoot him for?"

1

Leno smirked and said, "Fam was doing a whole lot of talking, but he wasn't talking bout shit, so anyway, what's the move for today ma dude?"

Block shook his head, took another hit from his blunt, turned back around in his seat, then said, "Well, ain't shit popping now cause of yo crazy ass with this Texas ranger gun ho shit; now I gotta call me a ride and the cleanup crew to come fix yo fuck up." Block took a minute to think about the situation. "I mean, the nigga was bullshitting, but he was still from the hood, you know; we grew up with this nigga."

"Yea, I know," Leno said, shaking his head, "but niggas gotta know we ain't taking no shorts or no losses, ya' dig."

"But it wasn't your call B, dead niggas don't pay they debts ma nigga," Block said, gritting his teeth. "We gotta be smoother than this; I mean, look at this shit." Block was furious. "LOOK AT MY SHIT! It's nine in the morning and this man brains is resting on the dashboard of my brand new truck." Block motioned with his hands. "A nigga ain't even had a chance to pass gas in this bitch before you go and do some shit like this. Not to mention, you making the block hot."

"Look," Leno said, as he ran his fingers through his hair, "ma bad ma nigga, but I couldn't sit idle and watch this nigga lie any longer; that shit had me vexed like a muthafucka."

"I feel you, ma nigga; it had me the same way. That's why I turned the music up on his lying ass," Block chuckled. "But it's a time and a place for everything. Now, how I'm gon get the 20 grand he owes me?"

"Shitttt, I ain't think about that," Leno said as he ran his fingers threw his hair again, something he often did when frustrated.

"That's your problem ma nigga; sometimes you don't think. I'm gon' change your name to quick draw McGraw nigga," Block said as they laughed.

Block looked through his Galaxy S6, trying to locate a number. He sent out a quick text and returned his focus back to his best friend. "Let me see ya keys real quick ma nigga." Block extended his hand in Leno's direction.

"Fa what?"

"Man, let me get them joints fam," Block pressed.

"Mannnnnnn, here dude, and be careful with my shit," Leno said, handing him the keys.

"I'm always careful nigga, fawk u mean," Block joked mocking DC Young Fly, the internet sensation.

"Yeah, whatever nigga, just don't scratch my shit."

"Aright son, I'ma get at you later; the crew should be pulling up any second now. I got a couple corners to bend," Block said as he opened the door.

Leno said, "Eyes open, my nigga; we may be good in the hood, but niggas is lurking and the streets is watchin', ya feel me?"

"I'm out bruh; you will get ya shit back when I get mine, can't be riding around with a body in my car. Make sure Adrian wipe this bitch virgin pussy clean, I'm talking Mr. Clean clean, ya dig?'

"I got you fam, holla at me later," said Leno. Block hopped in the old school Monte Carlo and peeled off, headed to the Anchor bar to get him some hot wings and blue cheese. The Anchor Bar had the best wings in New York. Hell, why you think they call them buffalo wings in the first place?

As he rode down Walden Avenue headed towards Best and Main St, he made a mental note to stop by his mom's house when he was done getting his food. *Damn, I need a haircut,* Block said to himself, glancing in the mirror.

Block knew he was sexy; women threw themselves at him left and right. Those types he paid no attention to, he wanted a loyal woman with sex appeal and an open mind. A woman who was independent but still knew the value of having a king to take care of her. He wanted a woman who could be corporate and hood when duty called. A woman he could build and grow with. Not a bitch who was looking for her next meal ticket and a good pussy pounding. Block was in search for a queen, his queen.

Standing 6'2", Block was the color of a chocolate god with a body made for TV. He had dark almond shaped eyes with long eyelashes, the kind that women paid the Asian chicks at the nail salon to put on. He had full plump lips with a tiny gap exposed between his two front teeth. He didn't believe in marking up his body; tattoos were a no go for him. He always felt as if tattoos were a way for a witness to identify you. Living the life he lived, it was a must that he remained incognito, if he wanted to stay out of that 5 by 9 cell.

Block decided that he would retire from the game for good by the time he turned 30; Leno could have that shit. He wanted to start a family and have a life without looking over his shoulder every step of the way.

Block may have done some dark and shady things in his past, but he believed that God would forgive him as long as he repents for his sins. The sound of his ringing phone interrupted his thoughts; he glanced at the screen and saw that it was Leno.

"Yo," Block answered the phone.

"Aye dude, some mail just came for you" Leno said, which was code for we need to talk in person.

"Word, just put it up for me. I will swing by and pick it up a little later."

"Naw bruh, I think this that letter you been waiting on." That meant, we need to speak asap.

"Aright, I'm headed back that way now; be there in ten." Block was annoyed, but he complied. Emergencies were emergencies for a reason.

"Aright one."

"One." Block hung up the phone, while making an illegal U-turn. "Damn, can a nigga just have one day without all this extra shit going on, and I'm hungry as hell too." *This nigga always got something going on.* Block thought back to the time when he caught his first body. As always, any and all drama in his life involved Leno.

As Block walked across the train tracks near Emerson park, he spotted a shiny object lying in between the tracks. As he got closer, he noticed it was a silver handgun with a black handle. JACKPOT! He thought.

Block couldn't wait to get to Leno's house; he fastened his walking pace. He had something cool to show him. "Leno won't believe this shit," Block said aloud. That nigga should have come to school today, he thought to himself. Block was so excited; him and Leno always wanted a gun of their own.

Growing up in the hood on Goodyear, all the older cats had guns. In their young eyes, that's what separated the boys from the men. Block and Leno believed that you had to have a gun to prove how much of a man you were. Being nice with the hands was cool and all, but to bust ya gun, now that was gangsta. Block walked on the front porch and knocked on the door of Leno's house and waited for Miss Trudy, Leno's mother, to answer. After what felt like 5 minutes of knocking and not getting an answer, it finally dawned on Block that she always left the back door unlocked. She didn't like anyone walking through her living room.

6

Block walked around back and opened the door. "Yo Leno, you in here!" he yelled, walking through the house. "That nigga must done fell asleep; he got the music blasting in this joint," he said aloud as he walked in the direction of Leno's room.

"Lenoooo!" he called out again as he opened the door to his room. "Wake up dude; it's too early to be sleeping nig... ga." The scene before Block had him stuck mid-sentence.

Block knew that Big Len was beating on Leno; he'd seen him with plenty of black eyes and marks on his body. But never in a million years did he think that his best friend was being molested by his own father. Stuff like that only happened to girls, he thought. What the fuck! Block's feet felt like they were glued to the floor.

"Shut up little nigga, quit crying like a bitch and man up; I'm doing this to get you ready for the real world nigga," Big Len said to Leno. "Life will fuck you in the ass with no grease," he said then paused, "that way when it does, you'll be ready for it." Block's face twisted in disgust when he heard that statement.

"What the fuck!" Block yelled, shocked at the sight before him.

Then and only then did Big Len realize that someone else was in the room. "Get the fuck out little nigga and keep your mouth shut; I'll deal with you later muthafucka!" Big Len looked back at Block, then continued his assault on Leno.

Block instantly became enraged before he knew what happened, he heard a loud bang resembling that of a gunshot. Block looked down and saw the smoking gun in his hand, then to Big Len slumped over lying on top of his friend. Paralyzed and unable to move, Block stood there shaking like a stripper. He remained in a daze until he noticed Leno trying to get from under Big Len's body; he snapped out of his trance to help his friend.

"Leno, you alright dude, you hit?" Block asked with tears in his eyes. He moved closer to help Leno push Big Len off to the side.

Leno looked at his friend with an expressionless face and asked, "Did you kill him?"

"I think so. I didn't even know the shit was loaded," Block explained. Leno was still shaking. He continued to stare at his friend; Block was concerned about Leno's mental state. What scared Block the most was Leno's lack of emotion.

"I always thought it would be me to kill him." Leno grabbed the lamp off the side table. "I hate that nigga with all my heart." Leno was filled with so much rage that he took the lamp and repeatedly beat Big Len in the head with it over and over again while he yelled, "I hate you, nigga!"

Block stood back and let his best friend release his anger. Finally, Leno ran out of energy and dropped to his knees crying; he released years of built up anger and resentment. Leno needed to let that out; there was nobody he could talk to. He tried to tell his mother, Trudy, what his father was doing, but she slapped him in the face and called him a liar. She told him to never mention it to anyone, ever.

Leno always felt he could tell his aunt Keisha, his mother's younger sister; he knew she would believe him, but he was too scared and too embarrassed to tell anyone else. Block calling his name made him stop crying. Leno stood up and wiped his face.

"Son, I know you needed to get that off ya chest, but we need to get a move on and fast. Ain't no telling who heard what; you know, we gotta get rid of the body." Block walked closer to the bed and sized Big Len up. "I'm too young to be going to jail; they gone tear my ass up in there."

Block thought about what he just said; feeling bad for his choice of words, he apologized. "My bad B, I ain't mean it like that. I was just saying, 14 years old in the chain gang with them old niggas. Then, they kill for sport. It ain't a good look for me son. But yo, what we gone do with his body?"

"I don't know. He's too heavy for us to move by ourselves; we need help." Leno walked back and forth, trying to come up with a plan.

As if a light switch went off in their heads at the same time, they both said in unison, "Keisha."

Keisha was the cool aunt; she was young, sexy, vibrant, and as gangsta as they came. She was 5 foot 5, long curly jet-black hair, and blue-grey eyes. She had the smoothest, most beautiful skin color; I'm talking paper bag brown. Keisha was the foreign baddie the rappers rapped about. She was a certified bad bitch, all about her money.

Her beauty was undeniable but, most importantly, she was all about family. Not having any kids of her own, she didn't play about her only nephew Leonardo (Leno). Although they were ten years apart in age, they acted more like brother and sister; they were just that close. Keisha never cared what the streets said in her eyes Leno did no wrong, or so she thought.

"Ayo, get Keisha on the phone and tell her get here fast," Block said with a sense of urgency.

"You call her nigga. I gotta get this blood off me; I'm starting to itch." Leno walked towards the bathroom in a zombie like state." "The numbers on the fridge nigga," he mumbled as he closed the door behind him.

Block walked in the kitchen to use the phone on the wall next to the refrigerator. He quickly dialed Keisha's number and waited for an answer. "Come on Keisha pick up, pick up, PICK UP!" Block said out loud, tapping his foot on the floor.

She picked up the phone with the music blasting in the background. "Speak to me."

"Hello Keisha, we need you to come quick; it's an emergency." Block showed signs of panic. Keisha sensed the vibe, turned her music down, and ask who it was.

"It's me, Block. Me and Leno need your help right away and please come alone," he rushed his words.

"Who the fuck is Block and where is Leonardo?" she asked with an attitude.

"I mean, it's me, Chauncey, and he in the bathroom. Please hurry," Block said and hung up the phone.

In ten minutes flat, Keisha was using her key coming through the front door yelling, "What the fuck is going on in here? And turn this damn music down. I can't hear my fucking self think! Where the fuck is Trudy?" Keisha asked, barking off questions and orders soon as she walked in the house.

Block did as he was told but not before saying, "I told you to come alone; who is this nigga?"

"First of all little boy, watch ya mouth; you ain't grown," Keisha put emphasis on the little part. "And second of all, this my man, Adrian. He good; I trust him."

"Well, I don't," Block said with attitude, poking his bird chest out. "What we need to discuss ain't for everybody, you know."

"Check it little man; I ain't here for all that and I'm sure whatever kid problems you got going on ain't concerning me no way. Watch your mouth when you talking to a grown man before I handle you like one," Adrian said through gritted teeth.

He ignored the first remark, but he didn't tolerate disrespect of any kind, so he had to put him in his place. Adrian turned to Keisha. "Keish, I'll be in the car baby; holla at me when you done with this kid shit." He slapped her on the ass and walked toward the front door.

Keisha shook her head yes and watched Adrian walk out the door. He knew she was watching, so he turned and winked at her, *then closed the door behind him. She licked her lips thinking about all the different ways she would ride his dick when she got him home tonight. Adrian was fine, tall, dark skinned, and bald. He put you in the mind of that model from the late 90's early 2000's Tyson Bedford. And the body, OH MY GOD, Keisha was getting wet just thinking about his muscular back.*

"So, what's this all about Chauncey," she said.

"It's not my place to tell you why I did it, but go look in Leno's room." Block was a little more relaxed now that Keisha's guest was gone.

Keisha walked toward Leno's room with hesitation, not knowing what to expect. The sight before her had her shocked and confused. "WHAT THE FUCK DID YOU DO? AND WHY IS HIS FUCKING PANTS DOWN?" she squealed in a hush like tone, just as Leno was coming out of the bathroom.

"Leonardo, what the hell happened in there?" Keisha asked with a perplexed look on her face. She noticed Leno's face was distraught, and he was carrying some clothing covered in blood.

"Block shot him," Leno told his aunt with not one ounce of emotion.

"I know that Leonardo, but what the hell for?" Keisha wanted a full explanation.

"He was…" Leno paused, trying to find the right words to say to avoid breaking down, but he couldn't find any. So, he went with the truth. "He was fucking me in my ass when Block walked in

and shot him." Leno let his tears fall free; in a way, he was glad he finally said it out loud to someone.

"HE WHAT!" Keisha yelled. She didn't really expect an answer, especially not the one she just received. She was shocked by what she just heard. "And where the fuck did you get a gun from!?" She looked directly at Block.

"I found it," he said, looking Keisha in the eyes.

"Found it where?" Her lips were twisted; she didn't believe a word he said.

"At Emerson park, but yo, we need to do something with his body. I'm not going to jail for this shit," Block said, raising his voice a little. Block felt like they were taking too long; he was ready to get out of that house and far away from the crime scene.

"I'm not gone tell you again to watch your mouth when you talking to me little boy," Keisha said with much attitude. "Let me go get Adrian. I'll be right back; y'all change them clothes while I'm outside okay." Keisha turned and walked towards the front door. "Leonardo, we will finish talking about this later sweetie." She had a sadness in her voice.

"Keisha, man, I told you I don't know that nigga like that mannn. I can't be having that nigga all in my business like that; what if he tells on us?" Block asked with an attitude. "That pretty boy nigga ain't bout that life anyway." That he was certain about; plus, Block wasn't too fond of outsiders.

"First off, I don't fuck with squares boo-boo okay!" Keisha rolled her eyes and neck with much attitude. "And second, that's where your wrong sweetie. He is very much about that life okay; he goes to school for this shit, okay!"

"To school for what?" Block was confused, wasn't no way they had a school for killers.

"To be a coroner."

"What's that?" both boys asked in unison.

"He examines dead bodies to see how they died, so never judge a book by its cover sweetie," Keisha said matter- of-fact. "He's the cleaner."

Present day

Block made his way back to Goodyear Avenue, the street he grew up on, to meet with Leno so he could find out what was so important that it couldn't wait. He pulled up on the block and noticed an unfamiliar car parked in the same spot his truck was just in. He emerged from the truck to meet a frantic Leno walking hastily in his direction.

"Dude, I fucked up. I fucked up mannnn; I really fucked up this time," Leno rushed, still pacing back and forth.

"Hold up B, calm down dude; just chill out and tell me what happened in the last ten minutes I been gone?" Block did a double take before he asked, "Who the fuck car is this?"

"That's my man, Pierre; he just stopped through here to give a nigga some vital information ya dig. But yo, remember that issue we had last week with the spot, right?" Leno waited for Block to reply.

"Yeah, I remember," Block said, never taking his eyes off the young cat standing by the car.

"Okay, well after we handled that nigga Jack, I had my little nigga Gutta get rid of the burner, just because I had some shit to take care of, right."

"Right nigga, just get to the point." Block just wanted the bad news; he wasn't interested in the back story.

"The nigga just got knocked last night on Genesee and Doat for a DUI. But yo, check it, the nigga still had them thangs on him, and it was the same guns we bodied that nigga Jack wit," Leno said in a hushed tone. "Pierre got a little cousin locked down in the county with the nigga who said the nigga singing like a canary bird right now, ma nigga."

"Word?" Block showed signs of frustration.

Anybody who knew Block knew when he was upset, he twists his Yankee fitted cap from side to side and spit threw his gap, just to calm his nerves.

"Question, ma nigga," Block said. "What was so important that you couldn't get rid of them thangs yourself? What was so damn important that you would allow a nigga to handle some guns that

15

could lead them boys back to us, huh?" Block twisted his fitted cap and spit on the ground.

"I was going to meet up with this chick I been tryna get at for a minute. Shorty bad as fuck; she ain't been smutted out like that or nothing, and she was finally ready to chill with a nigga," said a smiling Leno.

"See, this is what I meant when I said sometimes you don't think ma nigga," Block said through gritted teeth. "You let the pussy distract you and now we got unwanted attention on our hands. Thank god this nigga don't know the scoop on what really went down or else we'd be fucked." He looked Leno square in the eyes. "And what this nigga want, a cookie or something?" Block pointed in Pierre's direction.

"Naw, he got wind of the situation and wanted to give us the heads up, that's all. Look man, I know I fucked up, but we can fix this shit ma nigga. All we gotta do is send our lawyer that way and we can have the nigga out before the sun goes down," Leno said, as if he had everything figured out.

"You better hope so, my nigga; fa yo sake, ya better hope so. Because if not, you fucked. Remember, I don't even load the pistol without gloves on, so it ain't my prints they got downtown." Block twisted his fitted again. "Did you even handle the shit from earlier properly?"

"Mannn, come on dude. I handled that shit with care ma nigga, trust me."

"Righttttt, trust you like I trusted you to handle this shit in the first place right?" Block was aggravated with Leno's carelessness.

"Man, I slipped up but, trust ma nigga, that shit will never happen again, that's on ma life," said Leno with confidence.

"Yeah alright," Block had sarcasm dripping from his voice. "Just call them lawyers; I'm a call Caption John and see if them thangs can magically disappear. And as far as this nigga goes," Block looked in Pierre's direction, "find out what he really wants; niggas ain't volunteering they services without a fee, ya dig. Quite frankly, I don't trust the nigga, but that's just me; that's ya mans and them, so you deal with the nigga. Don't disclose shit about our operation to this nigga, just listen and watch. His true intentions will show; they always do." Block turned to walk back to his vehicle. "Holla at me when you really handle that ma nigga, and remember what I said!" he yelled over his shoulder.

Block searched his pocket for his phone; he had to make a call. He located the number he was searching for and pressed send. "Caption John's extension please," Block said in his most professional voice.

"May I ask who's calling please?" the receptionist asked.

"Yes, tell him Chauncey McCrae is on the line please, ma'am."

"Certainly, one moment please, sir."

Block looked through his rearview mirror while waiting for Captain John to come on the line. *"I really don't trust that nigga,"* he said to himself, eyeing Pierre. He pulled away and headed back towards the Anchor Bar.

"Chauncey, how are you, son?" asked Captain John.

"Spare me the formalities John and have yo ass at the Anchor Bar in fifteen minutes," Block spat.

"Well, what crawled up your ass son? Last time I checked, you and me were straight, weren't we?"

"Yeah, we good, but I ain't forgot about what went down last time either, so have yo ass up there in fifteen minutes like I said," Block said, then disconnected the call.

He rubbed his temples; he wasn't sure if he was getting a hunger headache or if the situation with Leno was getting to him. Quite frankly, Block was sick of cleaning up behind Leno, but he could never turn his back on his most loyal soldier and best friend. *This nigga gone be the death of me, but that's ma nigga though,* Block laughed to himself. "This old bastard better be there when I get there too; ain't nobody got time to be waiting on his foot dragging ass," he stated.

His phone chimed, indicating he had a text message.

Leno: *WYD?*

Block: *Im headed to meeting what's up?*

Leno: *The couple from before is back to look at the house again, they want to sign the lease today if possible.*

Block: *Great, let them know we can meet up at my office to sign the lease and to bring the deposit.*

Leno: *Will do glad we were able to rent out that unit.*

Block: *Me too, im pulling up to my meeting let me get back with u, good job ma dude.*

No one would ever know that they were discussing the Gutta situation, based on their messages. Leno informed Block that the lawyers were at the jail ready to sign Gutta out. They wanted to be sure they were clear to post his bail and that they would be fully reimbursed. Block gave the okay for them to do so and requested that they bring Gutta with them when they came to pick up their money. Speaking in code was a must for Block. He knew too many niggas that got sent up the river for having loose lips over the phone.

As Block pulled into the Anchor Bar parking lot, he spotted Captain John's City issued Chevy Tahoe. *His ass better had been here; I can't stand that pussy ass nigga,* he thought to himself. Block parked in an available spot, got out the car, and proceeded to walk in the building. When he entered the bar, he was greeted by a hostess with a cute face and a *phat* ass. Block made a mental note to himself to get her number after he handled his business.

"Hi, welcome to the Anchor Bar, pick up or dine in?" asked the waitress Brittany, according to her name tag.

"Dine in ma, but I'll seat myself; I see who I'm here to meet."

"Oh okay, well let me know if you need anything," Brittany said with a thirsty look on her face.

"I most definitely will," Block said, winking his eye at her before he walked in the direction of Captain John's table. Business was business and pussy never came before that; he would just have to holla at shorty later.

Captain John rose to his feet when he saw Block approaching his table. "How's it going son?" John asked, extending his hand for a shake.

Block accepted his hand with a firm squeeze and through gritted teeth, he stated, "Stop calling me that; you're no father of mine nigga," all while keeping a smile on his face, just in case they had an audience.

"Well, let's order, shall we? I'm famished," said John while massaging his hand and taking his seat.

"Yeah, let's do that. I'm jive hungry too," Block said, calling over the hostess Brittany, who just so happened to have been looking in their direction. "Say ma, do you mind getting our waitress? We're ready to order."

"Oh, I can take you order," she said, all too eager to help.

"That's what's up, then, I'll have a 10-piece wing and fry, hot with blue cheese, and a Pepsi," Block said.

"Okay, and for you, sir?" Brittany asked, looking at John while jotting down Block's order on her notepad.

"I will have a chicken salad and a Sprite; I'm trying to watch my figure," John replied, while rubbing his belly and laughing.

Brittany smiled politely, told them it would be fifteen minutes, and walked away headed toward the bar register to put in their order.

Block watched her walk away; he could have sworn he saw her put a little extra switch in her walk. Her ass was swaying back and forth like an ocean. *"Got damn that ass phat,"* he said to himself.

"So, what's this about Chauncey?" Captain John asked with an inquisitive look on his face. John was low-key worried; he knew what Block was capable of and he didn't want to be on his radar. He honestly thought it was concerning that time he allowed his men to raid one of Block's spots, knowing they had a mutual agreement that he was being paid handsomely for. Some of the men even stole from Block and the items they stole never made it to the evidence room.

"One of my man's soldiers got knocked last night. They caught him for a DUI, but he also had guns on him; those guns belong to someone I know. I need you to make those guns go away," Block stated, getting comfortable in his seat.

Captain John replied with a laugh, "You said that like that's an easy task to handle. How do you expect me to just walk into the evidence room and remove some weapons that's been bagged and tagged already?"

21

"I don't care how you do it, you fat fuck, just get it done," Block stated in a hushed but firm tone. "Need I remind you that you broke our little agreement when you allowed your crooked ass crew to shake down my shit and steal from me. I allowed them niggas to breathe on the strength that you asked me to spare their lives, but that shit comes with a cost. I told you that you owe me and now it's time to pay your dues. And, furthermore, we're not even until I say we're even, so don't even think about asking me that shit. Y'all hit my most lucrative trap nigga; 1 million cash and 20 keys ain't chump change nigga."

Block was getting pissed just talking about what happened. "I can't just turn a blind eye to that shit. The way I see it nigga, you gone be paying me til yo grandkids have grandkids, you feel me. And unless you want niggas' bodies to turn up at the foot of Ferry, you WILL do WHAT I say WHEN I say! You got that Captain," Block said with a scowl on his face.

"Yeah, I got it." Captain John was visibly shaken. "I'll get right on it."

"Good," Block said, standing up from the table "I'm a get my shit to go; call me when it's done." He left Captain John sitting there to tend to his own thoughts. Walking in the direction of the waitress, he asked for his order to be put in a to-go bag. She walked off in the direction of the kitchen.

Returning moments later, she said, "I put you some wet wipes in the bag as well."

"Good looking, I like things that get my hands wet," Block said, giving her a sexy smile and handing her a twenty-dollar bill.

Clearing her throat, she said, "I have something that gets far wetter than that."

"I'm definitely tryna see what that be like; what time you get off?"

"Eight o' clock, why, you trying to get to know me?" She handed Block a piece of paper out of her pocket.

"Damn, you was ready for a nigga huh?" Block chuckled. "But nah, I'm tryna see how wet it gets."

"So, that's all you want from me?" Brittany stated with a disgusted look on her face.

"Shit, I'm just following yo lead ma. I made a statement, but you took it and ran with it. Shit, I thought you was with it, but I'm not one for confrontation, so you have a good day ma." Block placed the piece of paper back in her hand, then turned to walk towards the door.

"Hey, what's your name?" asked Brittany.

"It's Block," he said.

"Don't you want this?" she asked, trying to hand him back her number.

"Nah, I'm good; maybe next time ma," Block said. He didn't do drama, especially with females. She flirted with him first, giving him the eye and all that extra shit. Then, got all in her feelings when he told her the truth about what he wanted.

Shorty bad, but I ain't with all that extra shit. Shiitt, she the one who came straight out with it. She might be an issue and a nigga don't need no more of those; I don't give a damn how phat that ass is, Block thought to himself, unlocking the car door. He decided to go home really quick, eat, and catch a quick nap before he went to make his rounds at the traps.

His headache was banging. Block was convinced that it was due to lack of sleep. He felt his phone vibrating and John Halkz talking about getting back home. Seeing it was Adrian, he quickly answered the call, thinking something was wrong.

"Ma boy, what it do?" Adrian said as soon as the call connected.

"Cooling, bout to take it in for a minute, what you know?" Block said, heading to his condo downtown near the marina.

"I don't know much, just wanted you to know all is well on my side of town," Adrian said in code, letting him know that he handled the Tone situation accordingly. "Your car will be ready in a few hours, ma nigga; I'll have ya shit delivered to the spot once its completed," he said.

"Cool, that what's up; I wanna have a little get together with everybody in a week's time. Let me know what day is good for you, ma nigga." Block covered his mouth while yawning.

"That's cool, I'm free Friday night," he said. "But, on another note, I believe I heard some rats near the Gutta the other night to. Might wanna pick up a few traps," Adrian said in code, confirming what Block heard about Gutta snitching. Adrian had a close friend who was a detective that kept them informed anytime their name came up.

"Bet. I'll stop by Walmart to pick up a few of them joints, but I'ma fuck with ya later my boy," Block said, turning into the underground parking garage for his condo building.

"Alright then ma nigga, be easy," Adrian said before disconnecting the call.

Block hung the phone up and took a moment to gather his thoughts. "Fuck man!" he shouted and banged his hand on the dashboard. "Could this day get any worse."

Leno

"Yo, good looking earlier on that info too, ma nigga. I appreciate it," Leno said, slapping hands with Pierre.

"It was nothing ma nigga. I'm sure you would have done the same thing if it was you." Pierre looked Leno directly in the eyes.

"Facts nigga, facts."

Truth was, he knew Pierre, but he never really fucked with him like that. He thought about what Block said earlier and asked him the million-dollar question. "So, yo, how much I owe you for that piece of information ma dude?" Leno peeled a few hundred out his wad of cash.

"Shit, you don't owe me nothing nigga," Pierre chuckled "I was just looking out for yo team, that's all. Like I said before, if you were me, you would have done the same thing."

But that's just it, Leno wouldn't have done the same thing. For one thing, he ain't fuck with the nigga like that and two, snitching was snitching in his eyes. So, him snitching on Gutta saying he is a snitch was just as bad.

And that's why this nigga is the brains of the operation, Leno thought to himself about Block. *He can smell bullshit from a mile away.* Leno laughed to himself.

During their come up, they decided that Block would lead the pack, since he was the most levelheaded of the two. Leno was more like the muscle; he loved to fight and bust his guns. Even though it was his father's drugs and money that put them on, he still felt like Block should run the show since he was more of a thinker. In Leno's eyes, they were still equal partners, one was no greater than the other.

"But yo, what's the deal with yo man though?" Pierre interrupted Leno's thoughts.

"Fuck you mean what's up with him?" Leno was ready to square off.

"I'm just saying though." Pierre knew Leno would not hesitate to put a bullet in his head if he said the wrong thing. So, he took the time to choose his words carefully. "I'm just saying though; he was staring at me like he was tryna read my soul or some shit. I was just coming through to shed some light on a few things is all; I don't want no problems with big homie or nothing," Pierre further explained his statement. Leno's eyes shifted and Pierre didn't want any problems.

Leno looked him in the eyes for a few moments, trying to see if there were any ill intentions visible. All he saw was a pussy ass nigga trying to play like he hard. "Ma nigga ain't to fond of new faces, ya dig. He was probably looking to see where he knew you from," Leno said, feeding him some bullshit. He would never tell him what Block was really thinking.

"But yo, I'm bout to swing by my bitch house real quick. Get at me if you need anything." Pierre was trying hard to end their conversation; Leno peeped it early on.

Leno opted to give him a pound instead. "Alright dude, I'm a holla at ya."

"You got ma number right?" Pierre asked, knowing he didn't.

"Nah dude, but I know where to find you if need be." Leno looked down at his phone, checking the text message that came through.

Keisha: WYD?

"Aright then, my nigga, be easy," said Pierre, opening his car door to get in it.

"Yeah aright, you too ma nigga," Leno dismissed him; he was preoccupied with his iPhone. He looked up from his phone when he saw Pierre pulling off, thinking to himself that he would keep watch on the nigga.

Leno: On the Ave, come scoop a nigga

Keisha: I'm around the corner now here I come

Leno: Bet

Five minutes later, Keisha pulled up in a pink old school Chevy EL Camino. Beating some old school DMX, *How's it goin' down.*

"Look at this fool," Leno said, smiling to himself.

What type of games are being played how's it goin down,

it's on till it gone then I got's to know now

Is you with me or what

niggas tryna give me a nudge,

cause honeys wanna give me the butt what

I'm getting at shorty like what you need what you want

Offer nothing cause' I got you, but you fronting

I see you with yo baby father, but it don't matter

Since you gave me the pussy that ass is getting fatter

"What's good nephew?" Keisha yelled through the passenger side window, while turning her music down.

Leno walked to her car and hopped in. "What up aunt Keisha; you doing alright?"

"I can't complain, just tryna maintain, staying in my lane; you know me." She laughed at her own joke. "Where the hell is yo car at?"

"Block got it but yo, run me by my house real quick, so I can pick up another whip." He grabbed the blunt out the ashtray.

"Oh okay, I got you." Keisha pulled away from the curb. "What you got going on today nephew?"

"Shit bout ta hit up these few spots and check inventory. Why, what's up?"

"Chill Smokey Robinson, let me puff a little nigga. I'm a pass it to you, damn," Keisha said, swatting his hand and laughing. "It's been a long day huh, man."

"Hell yeah, shit was crazy." Leno laughed, running his hands through his wild hair. "Run me through McDonald's drive-thru real quick; I'm hungry as hell."

"What happened today?" Keisha asked and passed him the blunt.

"Shittt, had to body that nigga Tone today mannn."

"Damn son, he still ain't pay up?" she asked.

"Hell nah and he wasn't either, nigga been holding out for over two months now. The nigga ain't even put nothing on it; I couldn't let that shit slide any longer ma nigga." Leno was getting mad just thinking about it.

"What Chauncey say?" Keisha asked, pulling into McDonald's parking lot. Which was only a few blocks down the road.

"He was tight at first, but he straight now," Leno said. "But yo, park real quick; I'ma go in. You want something?"

"Yeah, get me a strawberry milk shake and a large fry," Keisha said, parking and turning the car off. She pulled her phone out, deciding to read a little more of *The Connect* by Nako on her kindle app while she waited. Samira and Boo reminded her so much of her and Adrian's relationship. Except, she was Boo and he was Samira; she didn't want kids at the moment but he did. She wasn't ready for marriage yet, but he was. He went to college to follow his dream career, but she was addicted to the street life. Yet, she couldn't see herself with anyone else.

Two paragraphs into *The Connect,* Leno was getting back in the car. "Here you go auntie." He handed her the bag and drink.

"Thank you." Keisha put the bag in her lap and drove off in the direction of Leno's house.

When Keisha looked over in Leno's direction, she became misty eyed; all she saw in his face was the late Trudy. He had her funny colored eyes and her slender nose. Leno's hair was the same as hers; long, curly, and wild. Leno even smiled like his mother, whenever that was.

Keisha missed her sister so much; after Big Len's disappearance, Trudy was never the same. Trudy began doing drugs and later died of a self-induced drug overdose. Leno was the one who found her on that tragic day. Keisha often wondered if that was the reason Leno didn't value human life. The boy was quick to pull a gun, and Keisha often worried that he would die in the same manner.

Leno was the only family she had left; Keisha and Trudy's mother died of cancer over 20 years ago. Her older sister moved to California after that and she never heard from or saw her again. Her father was deported back to Brazil when she was a small child; Keisha had no idea if he was even still alive.

For as long as she could remember, it was always her and Trudy, and then Leonardo was born and that was all she needed. She wondered if he ever thought about his mother. They never talked about Trudy and, when they did, Leno would always get mad and change the subject.

"Do you ever think about her?" Keisha asked, wiping a lonely tear with her free hand.

Leno took a deep breath. "Every day."

"How come you never talk about her, Leonardo? I'm starting to think you don't miss her." Keisha looked over at him.

Taking time to chew his food before he spoke, "What's there to talk about? Talking about her ain't gone bring her back, now is it Keisha! Every time I think about her, all I can think about is the day I found her like that man. And that's some shit I'm trying hard to forget. Talking doesn't help me; it pisses me off and makes me want to bring her ass back to life and kill her my damn self." He threw the remainder of his sandwich bag in the back on the floor.

"How could you say something like that Leonardo; she was your mother, boy! And, as you can see, you only get one; you will not speak about my beloved sister that way!" Keisha said, a little too over dramatic for his liking.

He was thankful they were pulling onto his street. Leno was ready to slap fire out of Keisha with all this extra shit.

"Look Keisha, I'm just bout to hop up out ya whip before I say some shit I can't take back," he said. "You know I love you and shit but sometimes, you can be such a girl."

"I am that, but I'm also human, and it's okay to feel something sometimes Leonardo." Keisha pulled up in front of his house. "I still haven't seen you cry for her yet; I'm just worried about you boo, that's all."

"I know you are, aunt Keisha." He took a deep breath. "But I'm good though, I promise."

"Okay boo, let me know if you need to talk; you know I'm always here for you, right?" Keisha looked at her nephew with loving eyes. "Do you remember what I told you when you were 14?"

"Yeah, I remember." Leno smiled at his aunt. How could he forget it; she recited it to him all the time

"Well, let me hear it nigga," she said, playfully punching him in the arm.

"You always got my back fa whatever, whenever, forever," he chanted.

"You muthafuckin' right! And don't forget that shit either nigga. Now, get up out ma shit; big daddy on his way home and I still gotta cook," she said, referring to Adrian.

"Man, you whack as hell fa that shit, but I feel you. I'm out this bitch," he said, getting out the car laughing.

"You just mad cause don't nobody wanna be with yo crazy ass nigga!" Keisha said, hollering out the window while pulling off.

"Yeah aight," said Leno, looking back and smiling.

Unlocking his front door, he went in the house to take a shower, smoke a blunt, and get his mind right. He looked around and realized that he hadn't been home in a few days. The evidence of a three-day old plate of spaghetti was on the table growing a little family of mold.

"Man, hell naw," he said out loud, grabbing the plate and throwing it in the garbage. He looked around for more trash to fill the bag up with before taking it outside. He sprayed clean linen air freshener in every room, then lit an incense.

After washing the few dishes left in the sink, he retired to his bedroom to smoke and shower. He had been so consumed with the block that he hadn't changed clothes in two days, which was unlike him.

He prided himself on how clean he was for a man. He had a fetish with looking good and smelling good. He got compliments from women on a daily basis about his choice of fragrance. He had a thang for that Jean Paul Gaultier cologne; the bitches went crazy when he wore it.

Leno couldn't stand a dirty house, car, or ass. If he went home with a chick and her house was dirty, he would up and leave. Nothing turned him off more than a dirty bitch. Keisha made sure she installed the art of grooming into him; Trudy didn't play that shit either.

He smiled to himself, thinking about the years he and his mother were close. Memories of her washing and braiding his hair flooded his mind. She loved to braid his hair in all kinds of crazy styles; her blasting music and cleaning for hours at a time while cooking. Those were the things he would think about when she came across his mind. But thinking about her would always bring him back to that weary day he found her dead with a needle in her arm.

July 2004

"Mom dukes!" a young Leno called out to his mother Trudy. "I'm going to Block house for a little while; I'll be back in a minute."

"Whatever little nigga, just have yo ass in here by the time them street lights come on; yo ass ain't grown nigga," said Trudy, high on heroin.

Truth was, she could care less if Leno came home tonight or any other night for that matter. Her main goal was to get back that initial high she had 6 months ago. Trudy was on a hunt for weeks for that good shit, with no such luck of finding it until now.

She heard through the grapevine that a nigga in Central Park had the real deal, that shit that'll have you leaning like a kickstand. She finally got her hands on some and she couldn't wait to try it. Him leaving was perfect timing; her high was wearing off from the bullshit she smoked earlier. A friend of hers told her that if she injected the drug by needle, she would get a stronger and faster high.

Trudy shot to her room, grabbing her purse along the way with her get high utensils in it. She wasn't sure how to inject it, but she'd seen more than enough movies to get the just of it. She licked her dry, cracked lips with anticipation of the high she was about to receive.

She placed some of the powder on the bent up spoon. Using the syringe to measure her water, she placed a small amount on the spoon, making sure she didn't cause the liquid to overflow. She lit a teacup candle, then slid it under the slightly raised spoon.

Watching the liquid boil with bulging eyes, she removed the candle once she felt it had boiled enough. She let the mixture sit for a few moments to cool off. Placing a clean cotton ball in the center of the spoon, she watched on as all of the dark colored liquid disappeared into the cotton ball.

After tying the belt around her frail arm and securing a firm hold with her teeth, she used her fingers to thump for a big vein, just like she saw it done on tv. Once that vein was located, she emptied the remaining water from the syringe and replaced it with liquid from the cotton ball.

Popping her arm once more, she took a deep breath and pushed the needle in her arm, eager to get high. Releasing the liquid from the needle, she involuntarily leaned over with a big grin.

"Shit," said Trudy out loud.

This was exactly what she was looking for. It was even better than the very first high she got. Suddenly, Trudy's eyes got big and she began to feel a burning sensation in her chest and throat. Her body started to shake uncontrollably while she foamed at the mouth.

Trudy died within minutes from a hot dose, heroin cut with battery acid. Trudy's last thoughts fell to her son Leonardo Dupree Jr; she loved him with every being in her body. But the love for a quick high took precedence over her love for him, which in the end caused her untimely death.

Leno made it home just as the street lights were coming on. "Ma, I'm home!" he yelled while walking in the house. Trudy may have been on drugs, but she did not tolerate disrespect of any kind and he knew that first hand. Despite it all, he loved his mother; he believed she would get past this faze. He was giving her time to grieve his father's death, knowing he would never return, although Trudy thought he would. He wanted her to give up the drugs and return to the bad bitch she once was.

"Ma, where you at? I'm here on time just like you said!" he yelled, checking various rooms around the house. He knew she was still home; he passed her car walking up the driveway. He assumed she was in her room sleep since she had not answered him back.

He knocked on her door and waited for permission to enter. She would go off on him for busting in her room without knocking first. After knocking twice and not getting an answer, he opened the door to see if she was in fact sleep.

"Ma, you sleep?" he asked, slowly peeking his head through the partially opened door. "MOM!" he yelled in a panicked state, noticing her body hanging halfway off the bed. He ran to other side of the bed, placing his head near her face to see if she was breathing.

Her skin was cold to the touch; he knew she was dead and gone. He searched her body for signs of bullet wounds or stab wounds, then he noticed the needle still hanging in her arm. He knew she did drugs other than weed, but he had no idea that she was shooting up.

He looked into her face with teary eyes and, for the first time since killing his father, he felt remorse. He knew that she was missing him when she first found out he disappeared, but he had no idea it was this bad. And to know that he was the cause of it all made matters worse. If he knew the day him and Block killed his father would eventually be the cause of his mother's self-destruction, he would have gotten him some help. Or maybe, just maybe, he would have done things differently.

When his father died, his mother did too; she just didn't know it. Big Len was her everything and he knew it; their love was one and a million. When he went missing, she forgot all about being a bad bitch. She barley ate, she barley slept; she virtually forgot about being a mother.

He had an uncle and a cousin he didn't know much about, but other than that, all he had was her and Keisha, and now she was gone.

Present day

Leno shook the thoughts of Trudy out of his mind, as he applied the finishing touches to his Dutch master. He needed to get high quick; he hated when his mind raced.

38

He walked through his bathroom to his closet to retrieve his outfit for the day. Grabbing a fresh pack of socks out the drawer, he laid out a pair along with his remaining under garments.

Looking through the hangers, he came across an original piece from "The Harris Collection", an exclusive designer from the town named John Harris. A red Buffalo Bills jersey with the illuminating Bills emblem. The shit was dope; the sign lit up when the button inside the shirt was turned on. He paired it with a pair of white jeans and a fresh pair of fire red Timberlands.

The crisp Bills fitted cap he picked out was overkill. The Bills may have had a losing streak, but they were the home team, so he would rep them to the fullest.

Talking with Keisha about his mother had him in a salty mood, so he planned on stepping out with shorty from the other day a little later. For now, he needed to get dressed and make his rounds by the spots. He just hoped he didn't have to body another nigga today; he would hate to fuck up a nice outfit on some dumb shit.

After smoking some and putting the blunt out in the ashtray, he walked into the bathroom to shower. He stopped to admire his body in the mirror; his muscular arms and back were covered in tattoos. He loved tribal art, thanks to his late grandmother Hachi, who was a full blooded Seminole Indian. His mother made sure he knew his heritage. Trudy was half Brazilian and half Seminole. Big Len was Black, making Leno 50 percent Black, 25 percent Brazilian, and the other 25 Seminole.

To say Leno was fine was an understatement; he was gorgeous. He was 6 feet 2 inches, 220 pounds, with golden cream skin the same color as cocoa butter. Leno had the sexiest grey-blue eyes, a slender nose, and a perfect set of porcelain white teeth. A full head of curly, jet black hair that stopped in the middle of his back. His only physical flaw was a 3-inch scar along the right side of his jawbone.

Leno was a beautiful mixture of races, a real masterpiece, and he used that to his advantage. He had a different chick in bed every chance he got; he never met a chick he wanted to settle down with.

He removed the remainder of his clothes, tying his long mane into a ball at the top of his head. He adjusted the shower to the correct temperature, turned on his iHome speakers, and set it to Kendrick Lamar on his Pandora app.

He grabbed his Jean Paul Gaultier shower gel and poured some on his loofah. Lathering up his body and washing the danger spots, he rinsed off and repeated the same process. Turning the water off, he stepped out the shower. Leno believed bath towels held a smell after one use; he preferred to air dry while brushing his teeth.

Applying cocoa butter to the parts that needed it, he then walked into the closet to retrieve the outfit he picked out. Pouring leave in conditioner into the palm of his hand, he rubbed it through his hair and brushed his hair to the back into a low hanging ponytail. After getting dressed, he sprayed on a few squirts of the Jean Paul Gaultier. Ten minutes later, he was dressed and ready to go. Leno put on his hat, grabbed his keys, cellphone, and pistol, then headed out the door to make his rounds by the traps.

Pulling out his phone to call Block to see which spots he had been to so far to make sure all the bases were covered, he located the name, then pressed send. Picking up on the third ring, Block cleared his throat before he answered with a groggy voice.

"Hello."

"Damn, ma dude, I already know the answer to my first question since you sound like you just waking up," Leno chuckled.

"Hell yeah, a nigga had to take a power nap; ma head was killing me, but I'm good now nigga. What's up?"

"Shit, was checking to see where all you been today, so I wouldn't go to the same places," said Leno

"Oh okay, well I'm a hit up the block first, then I'm a slide through Ivy real quick, then we can touch base afterwards."

"Okay, well, I'll meet you there after I hit up the storage first. You tryna step out tonight or what, nigga? We ain't did that in a while," said Leno while getting in the car.

"Hell naw, not really, but I guess I will for a little while. Where you tryna go?" Block asked.

"Shiddd, the Oak Room I guess. But, I'll let you know," Leno said.

"Well, holla at me when you on yo way to Ivy, ma nigga."

"Aight then fam, see you in a minute," said Leno, ending the call.

Pulling off in his all-white Range Rover, he plugged in his phone charger and aux cord and selected Jay Z on his Pandora app. He always listened to Jay Z on his way to go handle business; it helped him get his mind right.

Driving in the direction of the storage unit they owned on Genesee and Union, he thought to call Esmeralda to see if she could wash and braid his hair later before they went out. It's been a while since his hair was professionally done. His aunt Keisha would get jealous if he let other females do his hair; she felt it was a good way for them to spend time together.

Coming up to a red light, he placed a call to Esmeralda to set an appointment for 6:30pm today. She told him that was fine and she would see him then.

He road for 15 more minutes before he reached his destination at L&C storage. Nobody knew him and Block were the owners, besides the people that worked there. They were bonded by a non-disclosure agreement, so it was safe to say nobody would ever know. He parked on the side of the main office building in his designated parking space. He liked to come in from the back of the building, so his employees wouldn't see him enter. He wanted to catch them slipping, just in case they were on some shady shit.

Using his key to open the back door that was connected to his office, he looked around to see if anything was out of place. Happy that things were the way he left it last, he put the code in his safe using a finger print pattern.

Block thought it would be more secure if they installed a digital finger print scanner that allowed you to select a 4 fingerprint pattern. He entered the code as thumb, middle finger, ring finger, thumb, then the scanner lit up with colors verifying his access. He removed his pistol from his waist and placed it in the safe between a stack of hundreds and few kilos. Closing and making sure the safe was secure, he then powered on the computers. Logging into the surveillance system, he first skimmed through today's footage, checking for suspicious activity. Satisfied with what he viewed, he selected the footage from the day before for the storage unit that he housed the dope in.

After 30 minutes of skimming through videos and being satisfied that his drugs were still safe, he decided to go make his presence known to his employees. Walking out of his office, he first made his way to the store manager's office. Knocking on the door, he waited for permission to enter. Although this was his shit, he still wanted there to be a level of respect. He didn't like when people just barged into his office without permission, so he made sure he gave them that same respect that he would want in return.

"Come in," said Michelle.

Leno and Block hired her as a favor to Keisha, which ended up being the best decision they ever made for the place. She quickly moved up from cashier to store manager, with her drive and determination. She was the first one to open and the last one to leave. Half the time, they had to make her take a few days off because she was always there. Michelle was the only person, other than Block, Leno, and Keisha that knew about what really happened at the store.

Stepping halfway into her office, he peeked his head in slightly and called out to Michelle

"Hey 'Chelle, I was just stopping by to speak before I head out; you need anything before I go?" Leno asked.

"Hey boo, come on in and shut the door; I was just finishing up some last minute things. I'm about to head out myself in another 30 minutes or so," she said, looking up from her computer screen. "You looking cute today, give me some luv." Michelle stood up with her arms stretched out for a hug.

"Thank you, you doing alright ma?" Leno asked while returning the genuine gesture.

"I'm good, you want a bottle water or something?" she asked, releasing him and walking over to her mini refrigerator.

"Yeah, I'll take one; how's the new guy working out?" Leno asked while taking the bottle of Fiji water she handed him.

"He doing well. Thank you again for hiring my cousin; he really needed this job," Michelle said with sincerity.

"Don't thank me ma, it's the least we could do for everything you've done for us," he said, meaning every word. "How are the numbers for the week?" Leno asked after taking a sip from his water bottle.

"Everything is as expected; 20 shipments came in from NY yesterday, I have one coming in from Texas tomorrow, and Florida will be in Monday morning." She was referring to the weed, coke, and heroin shipments Leno was expecting.

"Good, well let me know if there is any issues ma; I'ma stop by the unit and pick up five of each before I go. So, you can remove those from your mental inventory okay, and enjoy your weekend off; that's what you got an assistant for ma."

Michelle rolled her eyes. "For real, you work too hard ma; take a day for yourself," Leno said while peeling off 2000 dollars from his band and handing it to her.

"Oh, Leno boo, I can't take that; yall pay me well enough as it is," she said, shaking her head.

"This ain't an option ma; take this money and go to a spa or some shit, whatever it is y'all females do to pamper yo self," said Leno while laughing.

"Alright, alright, but I still need to come in tomorrow to oversee that shipment that's coming in from Texas," she said, looking him in the eyes while taking the money.

"That's right. Well, I'll do it. What time does it arrive?" he asked, reaching for his phone in his pocket to set the alarm.

"The U-Haul will be here by 12 noon, no later than 12:30. Anything after is a grand off a brick a minute for us, so you know they gone be here on time," said Michelle with a slight chuckle.

"Hell yeah," Leno said while laughing, "it will keep them niggas from taking they sweet ass time."

"Alright, well, I guess I will see y'all Monday then, bright and early," Michelle said, smiling to herself. "They having a party at the Oak Room for my cousin, Tonya, tonight; I guess I can partake in a turn up or two," she said while twerking.

He watched her ass bounced up and down, shaking his head. Lil mama had an ass, but she was off limits; she was practically family, being Keisha's best friend and all. But, she was fine as fuck. *She could definitely get it if she wanted it,* Leno thought to himself.

"Well, enjoy yourself tonight. I might stop through there since me and Block gone be in the wind anyways tonight," he said, briefly giving her another hug. "If not, then I'll touch bases with you tomorrow morning alright," said Leno, walking towards the door.

"Alright boo and thanks again," she said, smiling and holding up the stack of hundreds he gave her earlier.

"No problem ma, you deserve it," he said and winked at her while grabbing the door handle to leave.

After retrieving his gun from the safe and securing his office, he got in the car to make his way over to the storage unit. His unit was all the way at the back of the property with 4 units combine. Each time the door was unlocked, it would send a mass alert out to all numbers listed as contacts. When the system was first setup, Block had it designed to where they could watch live footage at any time from their phone. So, each time the door was accessed or an attempt was made to access, it would send off an alert to his, Leno, Keisha, and Michelle's phone. So, they would know every time it was opened. Michelle only went in when shipments first arrived to put the dope up herself and make sure the product was all there.

Leno unlocked the door using his key and thumbprint to gain access. Once that was done, he had 30 seconds to get his vehicle in the unit before the door automatically closed behind him. Loading up 5 kilos of coke and heroine each, he grabbed 5 pounds of OG Kush and two large zip lock bags of ecstasy to load into his secret compartment in the trunk.

Once that was all loaded, he made his way over to Ivy street to meet Block, so everything could be distributed to the correct trap houses.

Block

Block really wasn't in the mood to be hitting the club scene tonight, but he had already told Leno that he would go, so basically, he was stuck. After the day he had, he would rather just bust a nut and just go to sleep. Getting up with Leno, disturbing work, and counting money had him extra tired today for some reason; he really just wanted this day to end, so he could start off fresh tomorrow. It was so much bullshit surrounded around one day. First the shit wit Leno and Tone, and now the Gutta situation. The lawyers said he'd be released tomorrow morning after court; they were able to get the weapons charges dropped since they couldn't produce evidence of him being caught with them during his arrest.

Now it's just a matter of when he's gonna die; he could never make moves comfortably knowing it's a snitch out here tryna bring down the empire. He would hate to body the little nigga, but it must be done; he could never permit this nigga to continue breathing, knowing he out there bumping his gums. Block planned on handling his ass personally in front of the whole crew to show niggas he was about that life, and to let them know firsthand what would happen if you go against the grain.

Block had to make a real effort to get himself together for the night's festivities; maybe once he hit the scene, he might feel a little different. Block was not a fan of crowds, and the club was filled with a lot of drunk muthafuckers. All he knew was wherever they went, he was taking his strap. This was his city and he owned this bitch, but he be damned if a nigga caught him slipping.

Parking his truck in the designated parking space, Block got out and looked at his baby for a minute. He was not the kinda nigga to covet material items, but Block had a thing for all black or white cars. His nigga, Adrian, was the truth. He had Block's shit delivered to the block earlier, and it looked as if nothing ever happened. He even had the shit smelling like that new car smell again; they didn't call that nigga the cleaner for nothing. It was a wonder that nigga Leno didn't break the window. Block was just tryna figure out how that nigga got rid of the bullet hole that was in the dash; he was gone have to ask that nigga when he saw him, cause Block was curious to know how he made that shit happen in 8hrs.

Locking the car door and walking pass the security booth, Block spoke to old man Joe and used his keycard to get on the elevator. He had a little over an hour to get dressed and meet Leno at his house. He liked to make a grand entrance, buying out the bar in V.I.P. and shit. Block merely just came to people watch and make sure his nigga was good. He wasn't too fond of getting drunk in public places. He liked to be on his A-game in the streets, and he couldn't do that if he was drunk off his face.

Reaching the 17th floor of his condo building, Block used his key to get off the elevator to his penthouse. His building was big on security and Block liked it that way. Everything past the 12th floor were penthouses, so in order for you get off on those floors, you needed to use a special key to get off the elevator. Once you step off the elevator, you entered Block's penthouse apartment. A three-bedroom open floor plan, with three full bathrooms, and a half bath in the hallway off the living room. A dining room, a den, and a bonus room that served as a gym; every room was black or white. The kitchen was a state of the art chef's kitchen that Block barely cooked in. It also had floor to ceiling windows with mechanical blinds and blackout curtains. The master suite was all black with a California king size bed, black foot and head boards, dressers, and carpet. His obsession with black ran deep; white was Block's second love.

As soon as Block stepped off the elevator, he removed his shoes and hat and carried them to his bedroom closet. Block didn't allow anyone to walk in his house with their shoes on; a habit he picked up from his mother, Cheryl. She believed most dirt and germs came from shoes and doorknobs. Putting the shoes back in the box it came in and placing the box against the wall, Block then removed all the contents from his pockets on the island style dresser in the walk-in closet. He took off all his clothes, except for his boxers, and proceeded to roll a blunt.

Smoking the blunt to the halfway point, Block put it out and jumped in the shower. After handling his hygiene, he walked back in the closet to pick out something to wear. Settling on a black Polo shirt and some Robin jeans, Block pulled a crisp pair of all black Timberlands out the box. He decided to wear his new Yacht Master 18karat Everose gold Rolex, with the all black oyster leather band; might as well put that bitch to use. Block wasn't one to wear much jewelry; a single diamond stud occasionally and a Rolex watch was the most a nigga like him would do. Grabbing his all black Yankee hat and a few squirts of that Gucci Guilty and a nigga was ready to skate. Block placed his twin chrome desert eagles with the pearl handle in the shoulder holster he was wearing. He grabbed his keys, leather jacket, and phone, then headed towards the elevator. Putting on his boots while waiting for the elevator to come up, Block shot Leno a quick text, letting him know that he was on his way.

Block hopped in the truck and selected Kayne on his Pandora app, and rode out listening to him, Jay Z, and Big Sean rap about their clique. He was feeling this track cause nobody wasn't fucking with his clique either.

Twenty minutes later, Block pulled up to Leno's spot and beeped the horn to let him know he was outside. That pretty boy ass nigga left him outside waiting for about ten minutes, only to come down with the same clothes he had on all day. As soon as he jumped in the truck, Block gave his ass hell.

"Damn nigga, what the fuck took you so long? It ain't like you had to get dressed," Block said, referring to his all day attire.

"Shidd nigga, I still had to hit the hot spots and regroup," Leno said, handing him a pre rolled blunt while laughing. "Here, spark that shit up, ma nigga; this some of that hydro from Florida I was telling you about."

"Hell yeah, nigga, a parting gift; hope you got two cause this bitch gone be a facer," Block said, laughing with a straight face.

"I knew you would say that, so I brought these," Leno said, holding up a sandwich bag with what looked to be ten pre-rolled blunts.

"Ma nigga," Block said, holding his fist out for a pound as he pulled away from the curb. "Where we going anyway dude?"

"I was thinking the Oak Room, Michelle cousin having a party. Plus, I told her that we would slide through there," Leno said before taking a hard pull from the blunt.

"What's the deal with you and lil mama anyways? I see how she be looking at you with the googly eyes and shit," Block said, imitating a female batting her eyes.

"Shut up nigga, ain't shit between me and her; mann, that's my aunt best friend. Keisha would kill us both if I fucked her. But she could definitely get the D with that fat ass she got; I'd fuck the shit out her old ass," Leno said, coughing and laughing at the same time.

"Damn my nigga, don't cough up a lung," Block said while patting him on the back.

"Shut up and drive bitch," Leno said, laughing at Block's last statement.

"Yeah, I got yo bitch, fuck boy," Block said while showing him the twin guns he had under his coat.

"Damn, ma bad, ma nigga," Leno said, laughing and holding his hands in the air like he was the police. "Niggas get some new heat and jump on shit," he said, continuing to laugh at Block's expense.

"Whatever nigga," Block said with a chuckle, then turned the music up.

Arriving at their destination fifteen minutes later, Block pulled up to the front, put on his caution lights, and got out. He was parked in the street in the right hand lane; he didn't give a fuck about blocking traffic, them mutha fuckas would just have to go around. Just in case some shit popped off, Block needed to be able to get in his car and bonk out. So, using the parking lot or side streets was out of the question. He walked to the door and asked the bouncer if he knew whose car it was parked in the spot he wanted. The bouncer said he wasn't sure, but he would find out. Block walked back to his car and sat there, waiting for big homie to return.

A few minutes later, the bouncer returned with some chick with a fat ass and a princess crown on her head. Block assumed she was the birthday girl and this was her party. She walked up to his window and said she was here first and asked why he wanted her spot. Block responded by holding up two crisp Benjamins, which she gladly accepted and proceeded to move her little Honda out his way.

Backing up so she could pull out the space, Block parked and got out. Flicking away the last of his blunt, he dapped up the bouncer and tipped him a hundo and told him good looking. Block and Leno walked in like it was their shit and went straight to the VIP area. Of course, that nigga Leno wanted to buy out the bar, but Block told him to start small and get a few bottles. Hell, it was just he and Leno, and Block wasn't drinking, so they ain't need all that.

Block sat on the top part of the couch with his back against the wall and people watched for a while. He sat there vibing to the sounds of K Michelle's Ride out; say what you want, but the beat goes hard and lil mama could blow. Block had been peeped ole girl from earlier looking in his direction. But he wasn't into gold diggers. Block knew she had her sights on a nigga cause he gave her 200 dollars for a parking space, but at that time, he just wanted her out his face.

They made eye contact, then she held her glass up to salute a nigga, but Block gave her a head nod and looked the other way. He didn't want to give her the impression that he was feeling her. Block planned on fucking somebody tonight, just not her. She wasn't really his type, ratchet with an ass load of makeup. He liked a woman with natural beauty; makeup was cool, but only as a compliment to her beauty. Not the kind that would alter the way she looked. He was talking about the type when you go to sleep, she look like Beyoncé, but wake up and the bitch looked like something out of Wrong Turn Two. Bald ass eyelashes, no edges and shit type bitches, naw he would pass on that.

He saw Michelle, the manager of their storage unit and Keisha's best friend, walking in his direction with a smile plastered on her face. Block wasn't stupid and nor was she slick; he knew what she was up to. She had just come from sitting at the same table with ole girl, but Block decided to give her ass the benefit of the doubt. But, as soon as she said anything about the ratchet chick and Block, he would shut that ass down quick, fast, and in a hurry.

"What up Chelle?" Block said, getting up from the couch and giving her a church hug.

"How you doing Block? I ain't seen you in a while," she said, returning the gesture.

"I'm good and yourself?"

"I'm fine; all is well on my end. I just came over to speak, didn't want to be rude," she said, looking over in Leno's direction.

"That's what's up, I'll leave you to it then," Block said, moving to the side so she could walk over to where Leno was sitting.

"Okay luv, good to see you; don't be a stranger now. You do own the place you know," she said, coming in for another hug.

Block returned the hug and decided to go to the bar to get a bottle of water. He gave Leno the sign that he was stepping away for a second and to keep his eyes open. Leno nodded his head, letting him know he understood and would be okay while he was gone.

Block walked over to the bar and ordered two bottles of water and a side of lemon to go with it. He turned his back to the counter, so he could watch his surrounding while the bartender went to go fetch his shit. Block had this thing with watching the door and not being able to see who was behind him. He didn't like people walking up on him, so he tried his best to stay ready. Block didn't have many enemies in these streets, but you just never know in this game.

He saw the bartender coming towards him from his peripheral, so Block turned around, facing the bar to pay for his items and headed back to the VIP area. He turned around and bumped right into the ratchet chick with the princess crown.

Now, Block was not sure if the birthday chick was part horse, part cheetah, or what, but just a few seconds ago when he was facing the crowd, she was still sitting at the table. He turned his back for all of 5 seconds and, boom, she was right in his face. It was like she ran over, or galloped, or something. She must have been a track star in her past or some shit. She was so close, Block had to move to the side a little cause his elbow was touching her titty and his back was up against the bar.

"Damn, ma bad ma," Block said while moving over to walk around her.

"You good, what's the rush?" she asked, placing her hand on his arm to stop him from moving.

"No rush," Block said, shaking his arm free from her grasp. "I'm just headed back to my seat."

Block wasn't sure if ratchetness was contagious, but he wasn't tryna catch that shit. Plus, he didn't like random people touching him. She sensed his disgust and let his arm go, but she just wouldn't let up. She asked could she join Block in the VIP, since it was her birthday and her cousin was already over there. He told her that it was a free country and she could do whatever she wanted to do and walked off.

She started following him to the VIP area. As Block was walking up to the section, he locked eyes with Michelle, who was sitting next to Leno with a stupid ass grin on her face. Block looked at her with a mean mug and she burst out laughing, but he ain't find shit funny. They over there poppin' bottles and shit while he was stuck with this ole run down ass bitch, following behind him like a lost puppy.

His days of taking one fa the team were over. They ain't kids no more and he ain't in the business of settling for the cute friend at best, just so that nigga could get some pussy. If Leno wanted to fuck Michelle, he had to work for that pussy on his own.

Block walked straight over to Leno and told him that he needed to holla at him.

"Yo son, we need to be out in like 30 minutes' cause I'm not about to entertain her ass all night dude," Block said to Leno with a straight face.

"Come on son, she ain't that bad," Leno said while laughing. "I'd hit that, from the back of course. The bitch got ass for days."

"That's her greatest asset son; plus, she too thirsty. She been giving me the eye since we walked in this bitch; hell naw, nigga, I'm good," Block said, joining him in laughter.

"Aright, let me finish this bottle and we out, ma nigga. Thirty minutes to an hour tops," Leno said, looking back at Michelle.

"I thought you wasn't checking for ole girl. What happened to that's Keisha best friend and she gone kill us?" Block said, mocking him and referring to their conversation in the car.

"I ain't nigga, I'm enjoying her company. She pretty cool when she ain't in business mode," Leno said, showing a rare smile and walking back to the table.

"Damn," Block said under his breath, as he walked back to the table.

He couldn't deny Leno a good time, especially if he was really feeling Chelle. It ain't often that he showed interest in anything other than a fat ass on a chick. So, if he was enjoying her company, Block would stay, but word was born. Ole girl was not going home with him and he didn't give a damn what Leno had going on.

It was something about her that rubbed him the wrong way and Block always went with his gut feeling. Most niggas ignored that feeling for some pussy or a fat ass, but not Block. He wasn't one of those niggas that was pressed for pussy; he had bitches he could call if he wanted to fuck and be sucked. Or he would beat his shit himself; he wasn't shamed at all. Hell, he was gone get his off!

Block had to tell himself several times to be nice to ole girl; hell, it was her birthday. But every time she made an advance or started asking him personal question, Block would shut her ass down. Times like this made him wish he had a Facebook page or some other mundane shit he could use to tune that bitch out. And to make matters worse, her breath had the nerve to be stanking. Shit smelled like hot ass on a cool summer night. Block pretty much just sat there with a mute mouth. Before he knew it, an hour had passed, and he was bored and annoyed with that bitch's breath and conversation.

No longer able to take it, Block stood up to leave. Moving to the other side of the table, he gave Michelle a hug and told her he would see her later. Leno looked at him with the side eye, like he wasn't ready to go, but Block couldn't stay a minute longer. He had to get the fuck up out of dodge before he went in on her ass. She was too much with the extra touchy feely shit. He showed her on several occasions that he didn't like to be touched, but she refused to respect his space. Leno caught his drift and told Michelle he would holla at her tomorrow after the shipments came through.

The chick just ain't have no chill; she had the nerve to lean in for a hug like they had been vibing the whole night. Block put his hand up to stop her before she came any closer and told her flat out that he didn't like people touching him. Of course, she copped an attitude and tried to shine on him, talking about that nigga was lame anyway and probably gay. Now, by that point in time, the nice guy shit had gone straight out the window, so Block laughed at her ass and told her it was that rancid ass breath, along with her bad makeup and rainbow attire that turned him off. Then, he reminded her that he couldn't have been too lame cause she was damn sure checking for a nigga. Block told the bitch that he was a king and didn't mingle with the peasants, then excused himself from her presence, leaving her standing there with her mouth wide open.

After walking away a few feet, Block turned around and told her to close her mouth before some shit fly in it, then proceeded to walk to the exit.

That nigga Leno laughed all the way to the car, but Block ain't find shit funny.

"Yo son, you ain't have to go off on shorty like that," Leno said, still laughing as they pulled off.

"Yes the hell I did nigga; her breath smelled mad nasty and she wouldn't shut up. I sat there chilling, not saying much, hoping she would get the point that I really wasn't feeling her, but she just kept going on and on, ma nigga. I'm sitting there listening to this bitch, like I don't care if it's your birthday. I was just tryna chill; you know, vibe to the music and people watch, while you got yo mack on nigga," Block said to Leno, heading in the direction of downtown buffalo to check out this new spot called The Jump-off.

"Damn son, it was that bad?" Leno asked, breaking out in uncontrollable laughter.

"Hell yea nigga, my soul left my body twice nigga," Block said, holding up two fingers and laughing as well. "Truth be told nigga, I still smell that shit; spray some blunt powder in this mutha fucka."

That was it for him; Leno was laughing so hard that he had tears coming out of his eyes and he was holding his stomach. He doubled over in laughter even more when he saw Block was serious about his request. He grabbed the spray, then let off a few squirts, but Leno just looked at him.

"I'm glad you think this shit funny nigga; hell, that stanking ass shit blew my high."

"Spark up nigga, I'm tryna get high," Leno said, handing Block the lighter out the ashtray. "I ain't feel right smoking in there; I ain't even see niggas smoking a cigarette or nothing in that joint, so I wasn't either."

"Yea, I noticed that too, ma nigga; that's why I ain't pull them joints out," Block said, firing one up.

"So, what's up with you and Michelle, nigga? I seen y'all niggas over there getting all acquainted and shit nigga," Block said, looking at him and grabbing the blunt from his hand. "Give me this joint, nigga; I need this shit more than you anyways."

"Oh shiddd, ain't nothing major, nigga; we just rapped a taste for a minute. Turns out, we got a lot in common. I always had my eyes on her, but I felt like she was untouchable because of Keisha. But, like she said, we both grown and if we do take it there, then that's our business," Leno said, smiling to himself.

"Yea, aight nigga, Keisha gone fuck both y'all ass up, play wit it if you want to. That bitch is like a Pitbull in a skirt," Block said, laughing at his own joke and coughing from the weed smoke.

"Hell yea, we'll have to cross that bridge if and when we get there," Leno said in a more serious tone.

"Well, just make sure I'm there when you do tell her, cause I wanna see this shit," Block said, still laughing.

"Whatever nigga," Leno said, waving his hand and focusing his attention on his ringing phone.

Come to think of it; Block's phone been dry as fuck all day, but it was all good; he welcomed the silence. That meant that he ain't had to deal with no issues or thirsty bitches looking to lock a nigga down on some selfish shit. He had a few chicks on the team, but he was sick of them hoes. They were bad bitches and all, but it was more like a business relationship. They sucked and fucked him, Block wined and dined them; the usual come up type shit bitches be on.

Block wasn't tricking like the average hood rich nigga though; he was a boss ass nigga, but he refused to spend 3 grand on a purse for an average bitch with good pussy. These hoes ain't getting shopping sprees and vacations or extravagant gifts and shit. He might pay a light bill, a month of rent, maybe a hairdo or something, but that was it. Block was saving that extra shit for wifey; ain't a bitch in this world that could say he tricked that kind of dough on her, except his sister, Charmaine, and his mother, Cheryl. They would always be his special ladies. Wife or not, Block always had them, believe that.

"Damn nigga, you good over there? Shit, I done called your name bout 3 times already," Leno said, just as Block was entering downtown traffic.

"Ma bad son, I was in ma own little world over here," Block said while switching lanes.

"I see nigga, you done let the blunt go out and shit; spark up nigga, I thought you was tryna get high," Leno said, passing Block a lighter.

"I am nigga, light it for me," Block said, handing him the blunt and the lighter back. "Okay, so what you know about this new spot dude?"

"Not much, I did hear through the vine that you can bring a gun in with you, as long as you pay the 500-dollar cover charge," Leno said, taking a pull from the blunt and passing it to Block.

"I'm bringing my shit in regardless, but that's what's up," Block said, pulling up to the front of the club.

"Damn, its thick out this bitch," Leno said, referring to the line of people waiting to get in the club.

Indeed, it was thick; the line was wrapped around the corner. Bitches was showing all types of skin, like it was summer time and it was like 40 something degrees out tonight. These hoes ain't leaving nothing to the imagination; they were just starving for attention, looking for the next come up.

We decided to chill in the car for a second to thot watch and get a good buzz before we went in. Block knew if they had a cover charge for a gun, then we would be able to smoke in that bitch. Block just needed to be high before he went in; in his mind, he was more observant that way. After about five minutes of sitting in the car, one of the bouncers came up to the window and asked him to move or pay for VIP parking. Block asked him how much and he said 100, so Block piled off 6 of them thangs and told him he'd be out in a minute.

Ten minutes went by before they decided they were ready to head inside. Walking up to the door and bypassing all the people waiting to get in, they paid the line skip fee and put their arms out to get searched. The bouncer, who came to the window, told him they were good, so he let them in. Block gave him a head nod in passing, then winked at the cutie in the pink dress at the front of the line. Her dress was skin tight, but she wasn't showing off all goods for the world to see; she just might be going with him tonight, and she ain't even know it.

They walked in the direction of the bar, stopping to slap up a few niggas that they knew from around the way. Looking around the club, Block spotted a few of his lieutenants doing it big and chopping it up in the VIP section. He tapped Leno on the shoulder and motioned his head in the direction of the team posted up in the VIP. Leno leaned over and asked Block what the fuck they were doing in the club, instead of the trap, like Block was supposed to know. As they walked over, Block locked eyes with the cutie and her friend trying to make their way towards the bar through the crowd of thirsty niggas. If she wasn't all in the next nigga's face when he was done with this shit, he'd definitely get at her later.

Niggas froze up when they spotted Block and Leno walking towards the rope that sectioned off the area they were in. I mean, them boys was living it up like they ain't have nowhere to be.

"So, that's the move now? Y'all niggas a rather be out here blowing money, instead of making it? Making my money to be exact," Block said to no one in particular, pausing for a more dramatic effect. "Tell me something, niggas; if all my lieutenants is at the club poppin bottles and shit, then who the fuck is overseeing the work at the spots," Block said, looking each one of his lieutenants in the eyes.

Boogie was the first to speak up, trying his best to defend their actions. "Boss, we been putting in mad hours in the trap; we just wanted to unwind a little bit, that's all. We don't want no problems B. Real shit dude, we ain't think you would mind that much; we got the second in command watching the spots. Everything straight; all they gotta do is call if it's a problem. They know that," he said with a nervous look in his eyes.

Block stood there for a minute and took a good look at his top workers, and Block could see that this outing was much needed for them.

"Facts ma nigga, all you had to do was come talk to me and shit would have been handled the correct way. Instead, I feel like y'all on some other shit; tryna pull a fast one on ya boy or some shit," Block said while continuing his stare down with all of them.

"Shidd, truth be told, we could have all came out and fucked up some commas together; shid, you see we out here," said Leno, looking directly at Boogie. "Niggas been getting outta pocket a lot lately, haven't they B?"

"Hell yeah, but it's all good. I see y'all niggas really needed that break, so y'all go ahead and enjoy y'all selves tonight; buy a couple bottles on me," Block said, pulling out a few hundreds and giving them to Boogie, since he was standing the closest to Block.

"But, let's get one thing straight. The next time all of y'all wanna go out like this and leave the spots in the hands of the seconds, that shit needs to be cleared with me or Leno first; y'all got that?" Block said, looking them in the eye one at a time. "Oh and this little outing is gonna cost y'all 5 grand a piece, since y'all wanna be on some sneaky shit, and my count better be correct tomorrow too or somebody's gonna pay with their life. Any questions?"

Everyone shook their heads no while keeping an eye on Leno, to make sure he was on some chill shit.

"Cool, now turn up niggas," Leno said, pulling out the remaining pre-rolled blunts he had in his jacket pocket.

Block then proceeded to dap his niggas up to let them know it was all good. Five grand wasn't shit to them niggas; they paid them very well for running the trap houses. If sales go up, so did their pay; they were pretty fair in how they treated their workers. And since they technically never did put that rule in to play, they wouldn't let it go further than what it just did.

They were about 15 deep in the club that night poppin bottle after bottle, so you know the chickens was flocking. Although Block had his niggas with him, he still didn't drink shit. It was not that he didn't trust them to have his back, but wasn't nobody gone have his back like he had it.

After about an hour or so of turning up and buying out the bar, one of the bouncers came over and said they couldn't smoke weed in there and that they needed to leave.

"Ma nigga, take a look around you, dawg; we ain't the only people smoking in here," Block said, standing so he could be eye level with this big cocky mutha fucka. Block was not a small nigga himself, so he wasn't putting no fear in his heart.

"Well, I don't know about anybody else, but I was instructed to come tell everybody at this table that you all are being asked to leave, due violating the no smoking rule of this establishment," said Big C the bouncer.

"Okay, for shits and giggles nigga, where the fuck are those rules posted, cause I damn sure ain't see no rules posted by the entrance? And furthermore, instructed by who?" Block questioned, letting that nigga know he wasn't dealing with a dumb nigga.

Block had a bachelor's degree in business management, so he was far from a dummy. His mother made sure he went to college, so he could have something to fall back on. He always saw it as a way to help him clean his money. Block graduated with a 3.8 GPA, so ya boy was hella smart. Mixing his knowledge of the game with his college degree, ya boy had done fucked around and created a dream team.

"Yo, what is this nigga talking about?" asked Leno, draping his arm around Block's neck on some drunk shit. By now, that nigga was wasted.

"This nigga said we breaking the no smoking rules and we gotta vacate," Block said, informing him of the situation.

"But we ain't the only ones smoking in here mutha fucka, you must gone put half the club out then nigga," Leno said, slurring his words.

"Right," Block said with a screw face.

"Look man, I'm only doing what my boss the owner told me to do, aight. I know who y'all niggas are and I don't want no problems, but I'm afraid I'm going to have to ask y'all to leave or I will be forced to call the police," Big C said, backing down a step or two to put some space between them.

"Police? Did this mutha fucka just say he was gone call the police?" Block asked, looking back and forth between him and Leno. Block's lieutenants heard the word police and they all began standing up on high alert.

"We got a problem boss?" asked Flip, one of the lieutenants.

Before Block could answer his question, the nigga Leno was stumbling towards him, ready to pop off.

"Look here, you bitch ass nigga, go ahead and get ya boss fuck boy. I wanna see the nigga anyway shit; I done spent a band in this bitch tonight and, after he get ma money, he wanna put me and ma niggas out. Yeah, go get ya owner nigga; he on some hoe shit anyways," Leno said, full of rage as he let the bouncer have it.

Big C the bouncer damn near took off running in search of his boss to convey the message that was given to him. Block took this time to address his lieutenants and see where their heads were at. He wasn't sure how many of them were too drunk to even notice that there was a problem.

"How many of y'all niggas strapped, just in case shit pop off?"

"Shit, all of us," Block heard one of them say from inside the circle that was forming.

"Okay, cool. I'm not sure what's about to happen, but this nigga mentioned the police, so just be on ya P's and Q's. Ayo, one of y'all niggas take Leno up outta here; he drunk as fuck and I don't need shit to happen to him," Block said to no one in particular.

"I ain't go nowhere nigga. I'm good, BELIEVE THAT!" Leno yelled from the bottom of the steps.

"Yo B, why don't we just leave before the law comes?" I heard Tank ask from the side of me.

"Cause we Goodyear nigga, that's why; plus, I wanna see who this nigga is that got a problem with us anyway," Block said, a little aggravated with the nigga Tank.

"Here come them niggas now," Boogie said, tapping Block on the shoulder.

"Ain't this about a bitch," Block heard Leno say from the steps.

Imagine Block's surprise when he saw the nigga, Geechee, walking in their direction with his security guards. Now, he didn't have too many enemies in this world, but that was one nigga Block couldn't stand. He couldn't even stand to breathe the same air as this nigga, let alone spend money in his club.

Block and Geechee used to be cool back in the day; he was one of the older cats from around the way that took Block under his wing and showed him the ropes in this game. He was like an older brother to Block, but then he found out this nigga was on some other shit when his old ass was caught fucking Block's little sister. She was 15 at the time and he was 25. That nigga did a seven year bid on statutory rape for fucking with Charmaine and the rest was history. He just came home a few months ago, but Block had yet to run into the nigga. Had Block known this was his spot, he never would've step foot in this bitch. Hell, he probably would've set this bitch on fire had he known a lot sooner.

"Long time no see, baby boy," Geechee said with a smirk on his face. "How ya sister doing?"

"What, fuck nigga!" Block said while jumping down the steps and getting in his face.

"Slow ya roll partner; you in my house, remember that," he said, taking a step back as his security guards stepped in between them.

"I don't give a fuck about that shit, nigga. Quiet as kept, I owe you an ass whopping for that shit you pulled years ago fuck boy," Block said through gritted teeth, taking a step closer to him.

"Yeah well, trust me nigga, ya time is coming," he said after taking a pull from his cigar.

"See me now, nigga," Block said as he rushed through his security guards and aimed for his face.

Block punched the nigga so hard, he dropped the cigar out his mouth. He tried to scoop Block up into a bear hug, but he was pulled backwards by his jacket, bringing Block down to the floor. The nigga tried to stomp Block when he fell, but Leno was right beside him, so he grabbed the nigga that pulled Block, so Block was able to hop right back up on his feet. Then, he and Block went right back at it; swing after swing, Block was tagging his ass. He was on hoe shit, so the nigga kept trying to slam Block, but his feet were spread apart and planted firmly on the ground. Block done rocked with the best of them, so he was going in on his ass.

Block's team of niggas outnumbered his, so it wasn't long before shots rang out. Not knowing which side was doing the shooting or which way the bullets were flying, they released each other. Block later found out that it was one of Geechee men that popped off first, but the nigga's aim was trash cause Block's crew was able to run up out the joint without a hair out of place.

Block pulled out his twins, ready to shoot his way up out that bitch if need be, but them niggas made a mad dash out the back, so they dipped out the front. Block took count as they were running out and everybody was accounted for. Tank and Duff hopped in the truck with them, since they rode with some of the other niggas who had already reached their cars and was pulling off.

The shit was crazy; niggas and bitches was getting stepped on while trying to get out the way of the bullets that was raining down. People was running and screaming all over the place; thank God Block parked his shit in the front, so he was able to pull off before the cops showed up, which he was sure were almost there by now.

"Yo son, that shit was like a scene from a movie," Duff said, as if he was out of breath.

"Hell yeah, niggas ain't know which way them bullets was coming from. I saw one of them fuck niggas drop tho," Tank said with excitement.

"Yo, shut the fuck up dude; I need to think. Shit, y'all niggas act like you ain't never put in no work!" Block yelled from the front seat.

Taking a moment to gather his thoughts and plan out their next move, Block grabbed his phone from his pocket and shot

Adrian a text and told him where to meet them. They had a code red on their hands.

"Yo, call a meeting dude; get all the lieutenants on the phone and tell them to meet us at the spot on Koon's asap nigga," Block said to Leno.

"Aight, I'm a shoot all them niggas a group text now," Leno said, taking out his phone to get to work.

"As for y'all two niggas, when shit like this pop off and we tryna get the fuck out of dodge, I need to be able to keep a clear head. And I can't do that with y'all loud talking and shit in my ear from the backseat," Block said while looking at his niggas in the mirror.

Block turned on the a/c and some Jay Z and rode out on his way to the spot on Koon's Ave. For some reason, it was hot as hell in the car and he can't stand being hot. Block glanced over at Leno and this nigga was all into his phone, smiling and shit. "Ole sucka fa love ass nigga," Block said to himself while shaking his head.

His mind wondered back to the cutie in the pink dress from earlier; shit popped off so fast, he ain't even get a chance to holla at her. Block glanced over at her a few times in the club and, every time a nigga came over to her table, she would swerve on they ass. That meant that she really came out to have a good time, not to shop for niggas or look for her next come up. She could've had a man at home, which would make hella sense; lil mama was bad. She was bad on some grown woman shit. Block wondered if she made it out safely; hopefully, that wouldn't be his last time seeing her. He'd never seen her before and, truth be told, she jive had a nigga interested. He definitely wouldn't mind getting to know her better. Tank broke Block away from his thoughts of pink dress and said that he got a text from his second in command about a problem at the spot.

This shit was really starting to irritate the fuck out of Block; today had been nothing but a series of unfortunate events and it just kept getting worse. He told Leno to shoot Adrian and the boys another text, telling to meet them at the spot on Wood Street, since that was where he was headed. Block knew that it had nothing to do with the law cause they had special codes in place for that and none was given. So, he knew it had something to do with a jack move; given the last time he was robbed it was by the police, so he wasn't sure who was behind this one.

Arriving at the trap in record time, he jumped out the truck with his guns in tow. Block ain't even cut the shit off; he just hopped out, ready to kill him a mutha fucka. Block was fed up with the day and he wanted a nigga's head for this fuck up shit; enough was enough. Leno called out to him, for him to wait for Leno to get the keys out the ignition, but Block wasn't tryna hear that shit. Niggas thought he was a loose cannon, but they had no idea.

Block walked to the back door, looking around to make sure whoever was just there wasn't still there lurking. Block turned the knob to see if the door was unlocked and it wasn't, so he gave the special code knock to let them niggas know it was them and to open up. Soon as the door was opened, them niggas went right in to bitch mode, copping pleas, but that shit fell on deaf ears. Block hit the nigga dead in the face with the butt of his gun and knocked his ass out cold.

After 10 to 20 minutes of trying to wake the nigga up, he finally came to; he went into a state of panic when he realized that he was duct taped to a chair. Block told Tank to remove the tape from the nigga's mouth and for him to start talking.

"B, man, I didn't know these niggas was gone try that fuck shit. I swear, man, just me explain man; just let me go," Los said as tears mixed with blood dripped from his eyes.

"What nigga you talking about mutha fucka and this shit better make sense or else nigga," Block said through gritted teeth.

"The nigga Loci came thru, talkin about you told him to pick up a drop and to let him in. I ain't think anything was wrong cause he part of the team man; come on man, you gotta believe me, man. I swear, I ain't know he had them niggas with him," Los said, nervous as hell.

"What niggas? You talking in fucking circles; spit that shit out mutha fucka. Who the FUCK was in my shit?" Block asked, bending down and getting in his face.

"He was with the nigga Marlon, man, Geechee little brother, but I didn't see the nigga when I first opened the door. I swear to God on everything I love, man, I didn't know the nigga was on some other shit man," Los said, continuing to plead for his life.

"How much of the work did they get nigga?" Block yelled out at Lo.

"Three packs of H and 50 grand dude," Los said, putting his head down.

Block knew the nigga was telling the truth; he was as loyal as they came, but he had to know that somebody was gone pay for this fuck up. Why he believed that Block would sent Loci to pick up a drop for him was beyond Block. Los knew that Block, Leno, and Keisha were the only ones doing the pickup and drop offs. He could see why he thought it was okay; shit, Loci been down with the team since the beginning. He'd been one of Block's lieutenants for about 8 years now. He thought the nigga Loci was straight; he made sure everybody on the team ate good, but Block was wrong. Now, he just needed to figure out Loci's connection to Geechee and why he thought it was okay to cross Block.

"Aight, aight don't worry about it dude," Block said, patting him on the back. "Yo Leno, did Adrian get here yet?"

"Yea, he in the car outside; you want me to go get him?"

"Yea and tell him to bring his kit; I need him to patch Los up real quick!" Block yelled to Leno as he walked away.

"Aight," Leno replied.

"Yo, untie him and get the rest of the work and shit up outta here; we closing down shop," Block said, looking directly at Tank.

"Fa how long B?" Tank asked, bending down to untie Los's feet.

"Until further notice nigga," Block said, looking at him sideways. "If you would have been in place ma nigga, this shit would have never happened; you should already know better," Block said, pacing back and forth while screwing the silencer on his gun.

"Man, niggas was just tryna unwind son; I ain't know niggas was gone choose tonight to hit up the spot," Tank said with more bass in his voice than Block cared for.

Soon as Block made eye contact with Adrian, he turned around and let two off right into Tank's chest. The force of the bullets ripping through Tank's chest and made Los fall backwards in his chair; one of the bullets slightly grazed his left leg.

"Please don't kill me, B; I swear, I didn't have shit to do with it man. Word, life, ma nigga I never stole a dime from you bruh; that's on everything ma nigga. PLEASE don't kill me mannn, I'm, I'm just tryna make it home to ma kids," he said.

"I ain't gone kill you Los because you admitted to your mistakes, but let that be a lesson to you, nigga. Let that be a lesson to all of you niggas; don't shit go down without MY say so. If that shit don't come from me or Leno, it ain't law; you feel me," Block said with a menacing look on his face. "I want y'all niggas to know that you will be held accountable for your actions."

"Now, this shit with Marlon most likely stemmed from what happened at the club tonight, so we'll handle that shit accordingly. But we have rules in place for a reason," Block said then paused, allowing them a moment to process what he was saying.

"Now, out of all the years y'all be rocking with us, have I ever sent anybody other than Leno, Keisha, or myself to come and pick up my shit?" Block asked, as they shook their heads no.

"OKAY, so why the fuck would niggas think otherwise? If y'all know me, then y'all know I'm a creature of habit; the only thing I change is cars and clothes. Other than that, I don't change SHIT! Now, I'm going to go out on a limb here and assume that this situation was just a onetime mishap, right? So, niggas will use their heads next time, right? So, if shit don't look or feel right, then call me and let me know; if not me, then Leno or if you can't reach him, then call Keisha. Between the 3 of us, you will get an answer. Now, I'm done talking; I'm a get up out of Adrian way, so he can do what he does best," Block said, turning to walk away.

"Oh, one more thing," Block said, stopping in his tracks. "I wanna see everybody in my chambers tomorrow at 3:00, and I do mean everybody, from the cook to the runners. I want the whole team present and, if you late, that's a grand."

"Hell yeah," Leno said, finally deciding to speak up. "Matter fact, for every minute you niggas is late, that's a stack. Since y'all wanna fuck wit our money, we'll fuck wit y'all's, and bring them 5 bands that you owe when you come," Leno said, bossing up.

"Aye Leno, I got mines now, ma nigga. Sorry about that shit fam, we just needed some chill time," Flip said, pulling out 5 bands and handing it to him.

"It's cool dogg," Leno said, taking the money and draping his arm over his shoulder. "Had y'all not went out, then we would've never laid eyes on the nigga Geechee. And we also never would've exposed the snake in the grass, so in a way, we owe y'all niggas. But, since y'all already owe us, we'll just call it even. But, y'all still gone pay y'all tithes tho niggas," Leno said, giving him dap and laughing.

"Word, but good looking out on having a nigga back tho, I fucks with y'all the long way," Block said, as he gave each one of his niggas some dap. "Last thing, then I'm a let y'all go; clear ya schedule for Friday niggas, we having our monthly meeting and you know how that go," Block said as he walked toward the back door.

"Hellll yea," said Boogie with a sly grin while rubbing his hands together.

They met up once a month to go over profits and product, any and all concerns and issues. Things that should be changed or new business ventures. Usually, they would rent out a suite at the Hyatt or the Marriott or any 3-star hotel in or near downtown Buffalo. Block normally got his man, Delwin, who owned Myrical Catering to do the catering for the business part of their meetings, them Hennessey wings he made be the truth. After they handled business, they would bring in the strippers and have a crazy ass party; alcohol and Kush all in the air, accompanied by legs. Block made sure his niggas had a field day.

Leno would always say slick shit at these events like all this pussy nigga and you ain't trying to fuck none of it. Block's only response would be that he didn't fuck with hood rats. Any chick shaking ass for tips was a rat bitch to him; he wouldn't dare stick his dick in that, condom or not.

"I appreciate you, ma nigga, for everything fa real," Block said to Adrian, as they slapped hands and gave each other a brotherly hug. "But yo, how did you fix my shit so fast? The bullet hole gone and you got that bitch smelling like new again," Block said with an inquisitive look on his face.

"Chill son, if I tell you, I gotta kill you," he said, laughing as he walked away.

"Whatever nigga, let me know if you need anything else," Block said, laughing at his statement. "Oh yeah, ma nigga!" Block called out to him as he was walking towards the living room.

"What up," he said, turning around to face Block.

"This will be our last time in this mutha fucka, so make it shine and patch that nigga Los up first before he bleeds to death," Block said with a laugh and walked away.

"Aight ma nigga, I'll hit you up when I'm done," he said as he was walking out the back door.

As soon as Block got in the truck, he heard Leno on the phone all caked up and shit, talking to Michelle. Block knew it was her cause he heard Leno say he had a good time tonight; all Block could do was shake my head. This nigga was slowly falling in love and shit and Block still had yet to find his queen, Block wasn't gone lie; he was slick jealous. But he was still happy for his nigga, Leno, nevertheless; he deserved to have a queen by his side. Block could only hope that she was real enough to deal with his crazy ass. Not long after, Leno hung up the phone with her and asked Block to swing him by his crib really quick. Block looked at him sideways, but he obliged the nigga, Block already knew where he was headed next.

Block turned the music up some and rode in the direction of Leno's house. After 20 minutes or so of driving, they reached their destination. Block looked over to the passenger side and that nigga was knocked out cold. He guessed all that bottle popping must have caught up with his ass. Block shook the nigga to wake him up and let him know they was here, but he wouldn't budge. After 5 minutes of trying, Block gave up and pulled off, headed to his house; that nigga would just have to sleep at Block's crib. Leno had too many stairs at his house for Block to drag his ass up them shits. All Block had to do was drag this nigga to the elevator at his spot; Block knew he should have cut that nigga's drinking supply after he saw the first stumble. The nigga still had his back at the club though, with his drunk ass.

When they finally made it to the crib, Block sat there for a minute to gather his thoughts. A lot had transpired in one day and he hoped that tomorrow would be a better day; niggas were getting out of hand. Block needed to find a way to restore order to the empire; he wasn't sure what had caused a shift in loyalty but, best believe, he would find out. Had he gone soft? Block knew he was not one to kill on impulse like Leno, but he would if I had to. Did he need to change his killing habits? Maybe, he needed to be on some ruthless and reckless type shit to get niggas to understand, that they dealing with a fool.

Most people feared Leno because he was trigger happy, and they knew this nigga didn't give a fuck. But Block valued human life; he hated to kill, but didn't mind torturing a nigga. See, when Block took a life, it was well thought out; it was easy to get a gun and shoot somebody, or get a knife and stab somebody. But it was not easy to sit there and rip a person's finger nails off one by one; it's not easy to make tiny slits into a person's tongue and watch them scream out in agony when the salt starts to burn. Most people couldn't stomach that shit, but Block was all about sending a message, and it was not to fuck with him. See, violence was always a last resort for Block; he liked to hit a nigga in the pockets. But if you fucked with his money, his loved ones, or his freedom, death was most likely your only option.

Everybody knew Block as the laid back reserved type a cat, not too flashy, always humble, but still deadly. Niggas knew what he was capable of but, every now and then, they'd forget so Block had to remind them. They assumed that Leno was the one to be feared the most, but what they didn't know could in fact hurt them. They didn't know that when Block and Leno first started climbing up the ladder in the drug game, that Block was trained by the Asian mob. They didn't know that they had ties to the Russian cartel. Block used to tell the older cats that would fuck with him when he was coming up to never sleep on me him, cause he'd make sure that it was permanent. A lot of them had to find out the hard way; niggas thought Block was pussy because he was quiet. But that was far from the truth; they said that real gangstas moved in silence and that's why he was always quiet.

Block grabbed his keys out the ignition and made his way to the other side to get this nigga. After finally getting him to stand up, Block walked towards the elevator. The overnight security guard, Shawn, saw Block struggling and helped him to get Leno in the elevator. He offered to ride up with Block and help him get Leno in the house, but Block respectfully declined his offer. He didn't need that nigga in his spot, scoping out his shit and casing the joint.

Block had to stick Leno in the corner and hold him up while Block inserted his key in the elevator to get to his floor. This nigga was sleep the whole time with his heavy ass. Now, normally Block wouldn't allow a nigga in his shit with their shoes on, but it would be damn near impossible to hold this nigga up and get him out his shoes. Block would just get the cleaning service steam clean his carpet if need be.

Once the elevator stopped on his floor, he laid the nigga down in the foyer and dragged his ass the rest of the way by his collar to the first guest bedroom. Block threw this nigga on top of the bed and removed his gun and shoes. He placed his items on the nightstand beside the bed and walked towards the door. Just as Block was about to close the door, Leno said to wake him up at 10:30 cause he had somewhere to be. Block just shook his head and laughed at him, then closed the door behind him. Now, ain't that a bitch; all this time Leno couldn't function, but the nigga was sober enough to put in a wakeup call.

Block walked in the kitchen to grab a bottled water and a slice of lemon; he loved lemons in his water. It was soothing to his throat and added a great taste to it. After downing the bottle of water, Block threw out the bottle and made his way to his bedroom to shower. He had this thing with lying down in the bed with the same clothes he been in all day; He needed fresh skin to go with his fresh sheets. After taking a quick shower, he set his alarm for 10 in the morning, so he could get that nigga up; Block's day wasn't due to start until around noon. Block took a knee and said a prayer for blessing and better days. Not long after his body hit the California king and them 800 thread count sheets did he close his eyes to count them sheep.

Leno

"Yo son, how the fuck you get in my shit?" Leno asked, jumping up in his bed.

Block was standing there looking at him with two pills and a bottle of orange juice in his hands. After taking a look around for a minute, Leno realized he wasn't at his spot; he was at Block's.

"Oh shiddd, my bad son, what time is it?" Leno asked while laughing and taking the items out his hand.

"Time for you to go hit that tongue, you ole stanking mouth ass nigga," Block said, laughing and walking towards the door. "It's a new toothbrush in the cabinet in the bathroom in there," he said, pointing towards the guest bathroom.

"I know where it is nigga; you act like it's my first time staying in this bitch," Leno said, getting out the bed and stretching.

After brushing his teeth and washing my face, Leno sat down and looked through his phone to see if he had any missed calls. He had one from Keisha and 3 from Michelle; he decided to call Keisha back and see what she wanted first.

"Hello, what's good Keish?" Leno asked, soon as he heard her pick up.

"What's good nephew; just called to make sure you were up for that meeting around noon," she said, sounding like she was eating breakfast.

"Yea, I'm up now; I crashed at the nigga, B, spot. I don't even remember us coming here truthfully," Leno said, trying his hardest to remember the last thing that he did.

"Damn, it went down like that baby boy?" she asked, smacking in his ear.

"Hell yeah, but I'll fill you in later on that shit," Leno said, standing up and yawning.

Truth was, he was tired as hell, but he had shit he had to do, so he would just have to take a nap later on today, if business permitted it.

"Okay, well, I'll see you at meeting at 3 today; we can chop it up after. I just wanted to make sure you were up and at it. We can't charge them a late fee if we late our damn selves," she said, stating facts.

"Right, see you in a minute," Leno said then disconnected the call.

He looked at the clock on phone and saw it was close to 10:30. He needed to get a move on it and fast; shit, 12 would be here before you know it and he couldn't afford to be late. He'd be damned if he lost out on money cause he was late getting to it. Leno grabbed his shoes and shit off the nightstand and went to go find Block. He would just have to call Michelle back on the way to the unit for the meeting.

Leno called out to Block, asking him where he was, and he said he was in his room rolling up his breakfast. Leno was right on time cause he sure could use a hit to help with the nausea he was feeling from being hungover. Leno walked in the direction of Block's room to partake in a quick smoke session. Even if he didn't know where to go, all he had to do was follow the scent of the loud that he was smoking. Block was smoking on some of that good shit; that shit smelled better than the shit they were smoking on last night.

"Damn nigga, what's that shit you smoking on?" Leno asked while sniffing the air.

"This here is called Africa, grown in the motherland."

"Nigga, you bullshitting; that shit ain't from Africa," Leno said, twisting his lips to the side to imply that he really didn't believe him.

"Real shit nigga, look," Block said, showing Leno a case with more of the weed inside.

Sure enough, the beautiful box said made in Africa with a sticker strip that said Tokoiya's exotic imports and exports on it.

"Who the fuck is Tokoiya and how is she shipping you rare weed and shit nigga?" Leno asked with interest.

"Man, this bitch is bad; she can get you anything you want, anywhere in the world for the right price," Block said, passing Leno the blunt.

Now, Leno was slick scared to hit the bud. But, the minute he did, it was like his nausea instantly went away. That shit smelled like some of finest fruit ever known to man, and the taste was amazing. Leno had to get his hands on some of that shit.

"Damn son, I'm high already," Leno said, passing the weed back.

"Me too, nigga, that's the one and gone; you can put it out doe," Block said, handing Leno the ashtray.

"Here nigga, lets ride," Block said, handing Leno a small baggie with some of the prettiest lime green weed he'd ever seen.

No lie, the hairs on that shit looked like a rainbow.

"Good looking out, my nigga," Leno said, giving him dap. "But, on the real, I think I'm gone need some rolling papers fucking with this shit," Leno said, walking out Block's room toward the door.

"Hell yeah, that shit got me high ass fuck. You getting dropped off at yo house right because I got a few things I gotta do before this meeting at 3," Block said, stopping to put on his shoes while they waited for the elevator.

"Yeah, drop me off at the pad real quick, so I can wash my balls and meet these niggas, so I can get this shipment," Leno said just as the elevator came up.

On the way to the house, Leno texted Michelle to let her know that he would get up with her later on, when he was done handling business. When he got in the house, he took a quick shower, threw on a sweat suit and a pair of all black 10's, and was back out the door within 30 minutes. They had a deal with the connect that, if they were late, they could tax they ass heavy, so a grand off a key for every minute they were late insured their shit would be on time. But, the deal worked both ways but, instead, they could charge them a grand a key for every minute that they were late. So, a nigga was burning rubber to make sure he was there by 12:30pm. Leno wasn't paying they ass a penny more than he had to; he hated to deal with these mutha fuckas anyway, but they had the best heroin on this side of the globe. They had been dealing with these Asian fucks going on ten years now. Leno told Block that they could get a better deal fucking with the Cubans, but he kept screaming that quality over quantity bullshit. So, Leno was stuck dealing with them mutha fuckas until he found a connect who had grade a shit for a better price.

Leno made it there with 30 minutes to spare. Seeing as how they hadn't arrived yet, Leno took the time out to text Michelle and let her know that a nigga was thinking about her. He didn't know what came over him, but he was beginning to think like Block more and more each day. The thought of having a woman to come home to every night was starting to look appealing to a nigga. Living the life he lived, it would be hard to find a woman who he could trust and be honest with. But Michelle just snuck up on him; she made him feel something last night that he'd never felt before. Honestly, it kind of scared him, and there ain't much it in the world that he was afraid of, but love; love was the number one thing. The first two people he had ever loved didn't love him enough to be there for him, like parents were supposed to be. Therefore, love was some shit that he tried to stay away from; those hoes ain't loyal anyways.

Her response to his text made him feel all warm inside. To know that he was the reason she tossed and turned all night, had a nigga feeling some type of way. She thought it was bad now; wait til he gave her ass that dick; she ain't gone ever sleep.

Leno would make sure he gave her all ten of those inches; the meat he slanging was U.S.D.A certified; she better know that. He sent her a wink and a smiley face emoji, cause bitches love smiley faces, and told her that he would hit her back later.

Leno sat in the car for a few more minutes when he noticed the U-Haul pulling up to the gates. He hopped out with his game face on and ready to get this shit over with. The sooner they unload this shit, the sooner he could leave and go get himself something to eat that would soak up this liquor.

"To what do I owe this pleasure?" said Chu, one of the connect's head men.

"Figured I'd give Chelle the weekend off, she deserves it," Leno said to the noodle and rice eating mutha fucka.

"Pity, I was looking forward to see her fine black ass prance around in that tight ass skirt," he said, high fiving his little sidekick.

"Yeah, what a pity," Leno said, gritting his teeth.

For some reason, that shit him pissed off. He knew she wasn't his woman, but just hearing this Asian fuck talk about her like that had him wanting to knock that stupid ass grin off his face. But, Leno kept his cool cause whether he liked it or not, they still needed those mutha fuckas.

"Well, follow me to the back gentlemen; I do have somewhere I need to be," Leno said, walking back to his car to drive around to the back storage unit.

Leno might have to switch shit up a bit and have himself or Keisha meet these niggas next time. He'd be damned if these low eye bastards ever laid eyes on her again. Leno ain't worried about Keisha, cause he knew she would shut they ass down quick. But, baby girl didn't need to be nowhere around they asses, from now on.

When Leno got around back, he told them to pull the truck up in front of the storage unit. Then, he instructed them to wait until he was done counting the product. After counting twice and coming up with the correct amount of 100 kilos, Leno secured the unit and told Chu and his flunky that they could go. He had a truck with the keys already in it on standby, next to the unit that they were to drive back to Texas in. As Leno was walking back to his car, Chu asked to holla at him for a second.

"Yea, what's up," Leno said, turning to face him with an aggravated expression on his face.

"I just wanted to know if you had any issues or concerns that you needed to address, seeing as though you made us wait for a count and that's not how we normally do business," he said as he walked closer to me.

For some reason, Leno felt the need to let him know that the subject of Michelle's ass was off limits, and that she belonged to him.

91

"Yea, as a matter of fact, there is. Michelle is my woman and I would appreciate it if you and your squinty eyed friend would refrain from discussing her ass from this point on," Leno said, looking him directly in the eye.

"Well, why didn't you say so before?" he asked with a light chuckle.

"But I'm saying it now, so what does it matter," Leno said, daring him to question him any further.

"Dually noted my America friend," he said as he walked towards his truck.

Leno heard him laughing and talking that ching chong bullshit. He knew he was talking shit about him, but he ain't say it in English, so Leno ain't give a fuck. Block, or Keisha, most definitely would be taking over this account. If Leno never saw their ass again, it would be too soon. It was his connect anyway, so he good with not fucking with them. He'd just deal with the Mexicans and Maxx, his weed connect outta NYC. Block dealt with the Russians; they served as their pill connect. They had a thing about only dealing with him.

It was pushing 1:30 in the afternoon and Leno hadn't eaten anything yet. He was tempted to call Michelle and see if she wanted to grab a bite to eat, but they had that meeting at 3. Lil mama kept running across his mind something serious; he didn't know what it was about her. But, she had him questioning his damn self; is it really possible to fall in love this quick. It ain't been but 24 hours since he got to know her a little better, so there was no way I could be right? That love at first sight shit was for pussies, so I was good with having a strong liking for baby girl. Truthfully speaking, Leno had never been in love before, so he didn't know what it was he was feeling. All I knew was she made a nigga feel good and that was enough for him.

Leno decided to stop by Checkers and grab himself an order of loaded fries and a strawberry milkshake. Keisha had him eating that bullshit. She been on that shit for years; it was jive good though.

He texted Block to see what he needed Leno to do before the meeting. He told Leno to setup the torture chamber for the nigga Gutta. He had no idea that they knew he was snitching; he thought they was having a meeting discussing his promotion to lieutenant. Little did he know, this was his last day on earth. Crazy thing about it though, Leno was jive excited. It had been a long time since he'd seen his nigga put in that kinda work, he talking years. He would miss his little foot souljah; he didn't mind putting in that work and he was a good runner. Crazy, right? How Leno could go from talking about love to talking about killing? Shit, besides his parents, killing was his first love, but that's a story for another day.

Thinking about killing had him in the mood to listen to Beanie Sigel; he had to dust off the old cd book to get that joint out. "He could feel it in the air" was his song of choice for the ride to the warehouse chambers; they had a point to prove and today would be the day that they remind niggas of who run this shit.

Block

After Block dropped Leno off, he decided to swing by his mom's house to check in on her and Charmaine, and see if they needed anything. Walking into his mother's modest 3-bedroom house on Elmwood St. reminded him of the humble queen who raised him. His mother was never the flashy type, even after Block became the man of these streets. He offered to buy her a 10-bedroom mansion, but she refused to live in a house that big with just her and Charmaine. She always told him to stay humble and to never advertise his money for everyone to see. She would say the loudest one in the room was the weakest one in the room. That's why Block wasn't the flashy type to this day. He always been the type to play the cut and let other niggas flaunt they riches while he stacked mine. Now, don't get it wrong; he liked nice shit, but he didn't like the attention that came with all that nice shit. You would never see Block rocking loud ass Gucci shirts and shit. A plain white tee and a fresh pair of Tim's was good enough for him.

As soon as Block walked into my mom's kitchen, Charmaine came walking in with her hand out.

"Brother, so nice of you to stop by; what you got for me today" Charmaine said, giving me a hug, then holding her hand out.

"Nice to see you too bighead, nothing," Block said, slapping her hand away and laughing.

"Yeah right, you know better than that," she said, walking towards the refrigerator. She came back to the breakfast bar with a bottle of water and a lemon.

"Whatever nigga, where's mommy?" Block asked, taking out a 10 thousand stack and handing it to her.

"She in her room reading her lie books," she said.

"What the fuck is a lie book?" Block asked, looking confused.

"Them damn people's magazines and such that be telling lies on celebrities, at least that's what she calls them," she said laughing.

"Y'all shot out man," Block said, laughing with her and walking towards his mother's bedroom. After knocking and getting permission, he walked in and sat on the bed.

"Hey mom," Block said, bending down to give her a hug and kiss.

"Hey boy, what you doing on this side of town?" she asked, returning the gestures.

"I came to see you," Block said while taking a seat on the edge of the bed.

"Yeah well, glad to see you; lord knows it's been a while," she said, putting the book down on the bed and looking at me.

"You and Charmaine are so dramatic; it's been about two weeks. I've been a little busy; I just came to see if you need anything," Block said, looking around her room.

"No sweetie, but thank you; how is Leonardo doing? Tell him he can still come and see his old lady from time to time," she said, looking at her ringing phone.

"One second son," she said, holding up her finger. "Hey George, let me call you back, my son is here visiting," she said before disconnecting the call.

"Who is George?" Block asked, soon as she disconnected.

"Never you mind child, now what were you saying," she said, brushing him off.

"Nothing ma, I'm about to head out. I gotta a meeting to go to in a little bit anyway; go ahead and call you little friend George back," Block said, getting up and pulling her in for a hug.

"Oh, come on Chauncey. George and I are just friends; plus, you just got here," she said, holding on to him.

"Ma, I really do have somewhere to be, I'll try to stop back by later on if I can," Block said, looking her in her eyes while still holding her hands. "Here, take this and get whatever it is old ladies buy with their son's money," Block said, handing her a 10 grand stack as well.

"We old ladies go to Walmart and ball out; that's what we do," she said, laughing and putting it in her bra. "I love you, son, and do stop back by if you can hun," she said after kissing him on the cheek.

"Love you too, I will," Block said, turning around to leave.

"Bye bighead," Block said, walking past Charmaine, lightly pushing her on the head.

"You gone already?" she asked, pulling the phone from her ear.

"Yeah, I'll be back through here later on," Block said, walking towards the door.

"Yeah, whatever nigga, be safe, love you." She returned to her phone conversation.

"Love you too," Block said before he closed the door.

He was on the way to his favorite eating spot; he was in the mood for chicken wings again. He ate there at least 3 times a week; they basically knew his order by heart. Truthfully speaking, Block could never get tired of chicken; he didn't eat pork much, so chicken was his favorite dish.

Pulling into the parking lot of the Anchor Bar, he spotted this chick; she certainly had his attention. So much so, that he damn near crashed into the car in front of him, waiting to park in a space near the entrance.

"Is that who I think it is?" Block said out loud. He couldn't believe his luck; he never thought he would come across pink dress so soon. She had an aura about her that he was drawn to; she ran across his mind several times last night, then to see her less than 24 hours later was fate in his eyes.

It was rare that he came across a female that caught his eye, but she was bad as shit. She was beyond gorgeous; a tall light skinned beauty with long hair and hips for days. Although she had on her work clothes, he could still see that ass through them scrubs.

"She gotta be Spanish or something damn; I hope she ain't just a CAN," Block said to himself out loud and laughing.

He had to talk to her; he quickly parked, got out the car, and locked the door. "How you doing Miss?" he asked to the slim goodie walking in front of him.

She turned and smiled at him. "I'm fine and yourself."

"I'm better now, thanks for asking," he said. She politely smiled back at him and continued walking toward the entrance.

"Hold up, let me get the door for you, ma," he said, reaching for the door handle, "a lady such as yourself will never touch a door as long as I'm around."

"Thank you, aren't you so kind."

"What's your name sweetheart?" Block asked as she walked into the bar.

"Chasity, and you are?"

"Block," he said. "Nice to meet you, Miss Chasity."

"Yeah, you too," she said with attitude oozing from her voice.

Catching the hint, Block asked, "Did I miss something here?"

"If you have to ask, then no need to continue this conversation." Turning her back to him, Chasity waved down a server. "Pick up for Chasity please."

"Yes ma'am, one moment please," the hostess replied with her eyes on Block.

Chasity noticed the thirstiness and just shook her head at the young girl.

"My bad ma, did I do something wrong?"

Chasity replied with confidence, "Other than waste my time, no."

Block looked her up and down and a smirk spread across his face. "What's that look for Mr. Hood, excuse me, Block," Chasity was irritated.

"Nothing ma, I just think you cute when you mad."

"Let's get one thing straight sweetie. I was never mad, a little aggravated yes, but mad, I think not." She dismissed him. "I mean, you came off as a gentlemen and you appeared to be of grown man status. Then, you commence to giving me a nickname after I gave you my real name. I am a 35-year-old woman who has not an ounce of time for games. Besides, I'm on my lunch break and I only have 1 hour to spare. So, I would rather use that time wisely, then to be bothered with the likes of a man who can't respect a lady enough to properly introduce himself," she stated with satisfaction. "Anyway, the young lady who was just here would much rather be in your face."

Block took a step back to compose himself, never had a female checked him in such a matter; truth be told, it was making his dick hard. "My apologies Ms. Chasity, I'm not use to being in the presence of a real women; can we start over? My name is Chauncey. It's nice to make your acquaintance pretty lady."

Chasity smiled and chuckled "You so extra, but it's nice to meet you too, Mr. Chauncey."

"Can I join you for lunch miss lady?"

"I don't see why not sir, but my food is ready already because I called ahead. And sorry to say, I'm not waiting on yours to be prepared cause I'm beyond hungry right now"

"You're such a freaking lady Ms. Chasity; that's fine, I don't mind watching you pig out," Block laughed.

"I bet you don't," she laughed with him. *Damn, he got a sexy smile, and those lips. Shitttt; I wonder what that mouth do?* she thought, smiling.

"What got you smiling so hard; what's on ya mind ma?" Block asked, smiling back at her.

Them soft ass lips. "Oh nothing, I was just thinking about something a patient of mine said to me earlier."

"Oh okay, what field of nursing are you in?"

"I'm an ambulatory care nurse," she stated proudly. Block looked at her in awe, even though he didn't know exactly what that meant. He knew she had to be smart though.

"At least she ain't say cna," Block thought to himself as he stuffed his hands in his pants pocket.

Chasity sensed his confusion, so she clarified. "I'm a registered nurse, but I work in the emergency room, also known as a trauma nurse."

"Oh, why didn't u just say you worked in the ER woman?" Block laughed. "Got a nigga bout to pull out the phone and ask Jeeves and shit."

"You got jokes I see," Chasity giggled. "well, I love my job; it is never a dull moment around that place, but what is it that you do Mr. Chauncey?" Chasity spotted the waitress walking in their direction.

"I'm a drug dealer," Block looked her directly in the eyes with a straight face.

"That will be $10.55," the thirsty waitress interrupted; Chasity caught her eye fucking Block.

"Here you go sweetie and keep the change." Chasity pushed the money in her hand. "Oh and for future references, you really should watch your wandering eyes because if he was in fact, my man, you would be wearing these buffalo wings okay sweetie."

"No man likes a friendly woman love; have some class and give them a bit of a chase. You will come out better that way." Chasity rolled her eyes, then walked towards an available table. Block looked on astonished and adjusted himself; that's twice in one day that Chasity had inadvertently made his dick hard. He smirked and winked at the cute little waitress, then followed behind Chasity to her table.

"If I ain't know any better, I would have thought you was feeling a nigga," Block smirked.

"I mean, you're a nice looking man, but in order to be *feeling* you, I would have to know more about you other than your first name and your occupation," Chasity said, taking a seat. "Speaking of which, do you just openly tell every woman you meet what it is you really do for a living? How do you know I'm not the police?"

"Because you already told me what you did for a living, and, furthermore, I know a cop when I see one." He helped himself to a fry from her plate.

Chasity looked at him like he was crazy. She didn't play about her food. "Are you comfortable Mr. Chauncey?"

"I'm quite comfy; why do you ask," Block said, this time stealing a chicken wing from her plate.

"Because you just reached into my plate and helped yourself without asking; how do I know if you washed your hands," she said, crossing her arms and sitting back in the seat.

"You don't, but how do you know if the person fixing your food has washed his or her hands either?" he questioned, taking another fry from her plate and laughing.

"Alright now, reach over here again and you gone pull back a nub." She joined him in laughter.

"Easy tiger," Block said, laughing while waving the waitress over to his table.

"You would call the thirsty chick over here," she said, rolling her eyes and laughing. "You, sir, are messy."

"I'm not messy. I would have called someone else but, seeing as though she's the only person available to take orders, I don't really have a choice now, do I sexy?" Block licked his lips.

"Touché, my good sir," she said, taking a sip of her lemon water.

"Be careful with that straw ma; you push it back any further and that bitch gone be down your throat." Block watched her every move.

"I'm sorry, my mind went somewhere else for a minute," she said, just as the waitress arrived at their table.

Block placed his usual order and continued with his conversation. "Now, where was your mind when you were swallowing the hell out that straw?" he asked, turning his attention back to Chasity.

"Let's just say it was in an ungodly place at that moment."

"My mind been having crazy thoughts since I saw your fine ass walk across the parking lot, but I'll keep them to myself for now," Block said, reaching across the table to wipe the sauce from the corner of her mouth.

Taking a moment to compose herself, Chasity looked up into Block's eyes; she couldn't deny the fire she saw burning within them. The feeling of electricity shot through her veins and out her pussy lips when he touched her. In all of her 35 years of living, she never felt a feeling like that before.

Just a touch from that man did something to her lower region, a feeling of undeniable sexual desire, that she just could not explain. Chasity wasn't sure if this feeling came from her lack of sex, or was it the power of his touch but, either way, she was bound to find out.

Block continued with his intense stare, never once taking his eyes off hers. It was as if he was trying to read her thoughts or look into her soul. Once again, they were interrupted by the waitress who returned with Block's food. Chasity welcomed the interruption; this stare down game was beginning to do something to her.

The waitress, Brittany, placed Block's plate of food on the table in front of him and asked if she could get them anything else. He answered no, gave her a 20-dollar bill, and told her to keep the change; never taking his eyes off the gorgeous creature in front of him. Brittany was the last thing on his mind.

Chasity reminded him of Diamond from the Player's Club, played by the actress Lisa Raye. Chasity was a light skinned, slim goodie with thickness in all the right places, not as tall but still sexy, nevertheless. Her almond shaped hazel eyes only added to her beauty, making her dangerously sexy in Block's book.

"Look, I have a meeting to go very shortly, but I would love to see you again beautiful," he said, still looking her in the eye.

"I would like that." She blushed and lowered her head.

"Let me see yo phone ma." He put his number into her phone and saved it under future.

"Alright, text me and send me your number ma." He touched her chin to gently lift her head. "Make sure you do that ma."

Block stood up and waved the waitress down. "Let me get a to-go plate shorty."

After putting his food in the plate, he looked at his phone to see if he had a text from her. "What's taking you so long ma; I told you I'm ya future. You shouldn't keep ya future waiting," he said with a sly grin.

"Boy, I will as soon as I'm done eating," she said, waving him off.

"I like the little smart mouth you got; we might have to do something with it," Block said with a smile.

"Boy bye."

"Alright, pink dress, you stay sexy," he said, walking away and leaving her with her mouth open.

On the drive over to the warehouse, Block replayed their encounter in head; he was baffled at his own bluntness. He didn't even think twice when he said drugs; it actually felt good to be honest with a woman up front. He could have told her about the staffing agency he owned or he could have said he owned real estate, which wasn't a lie. He did own all the houses they trapped out of. But, for some reason, he felt compelled to tell her the truth, that way she could come to the conclusion of whether or not she wanted to deal with him on her own. He would hate for them to get deep into the relationship and she found out what he really did and decide that she couldn't deal with it. She had him feeling out of his element; he wasn't a shy man by a long shot, but he was never this straight forward about his feelings when it came to women either. It was if he was having an out of body experience and his heart was telling him that she was the one.

When he touched her face, his heart rate picked up; he was drawn to her and he had no idea why. He had been in the presence of many beautiful women, but he felt like her beauty was unmatched. She had a way of drawing you in, like a pig to mud or a fly to shit; he simply was drawn to her. He wondered how a person could make that assumption or feel that way after 30 minutes of conversation, but he was blessed with discernment and he always trusted his gut. Something told him that he needed to get to know her better, that she would be just what he needed, and to be honest with her. Hell, the way she shut him down after he gave her his nickname, he knew then that shorty was a force to be reckoned with; he made up his mind right then to start off with the truth.

He looked at his ringing phone just as he was pulling in to the warehouse parking lot. It was a number he didn't recognize; he was just about to send it to voicemail when he realized it might be her.

"Hello," he answered as he pulled into his designated parking space.

"Hi future, I was just making sure you had the number," Chasity said with a present smile in her voice.

"Hey futuress, bout time you called; a nigga was beginning to think you was running from your destiny," Block said with a laugh.

"You so sure of yourself hun, Mr. Future," she said

"That I am, I'm just waiting on you to realize it," he said while putting the car in park and turning it off.

"We will certainly see what the future holds; the thing with the future is that you never know what it will be" she said, feeling proud of her quick comeback.

"Oh, I know what your future looks like," he said with a pause. "And it's me," he said with a smile, getting out of the car with his food in hand.

"Well, we shall see Mr. Future, but I won't hold you up. I know you have a meeting to attend, and I must get back to work," she said.

"Okay beautiful, you enjoy the rest of your day and feel free to call me when you get off; use this time to prepare for your future," he said with a slight chuckle, just as he was walking into his office.

"You so extra, but you do the same sir," she said, just before she disconnected the call.

Block shook his head as he removed his phone from his ear. Her smart mouth was a major turn on for him; to him that meant she wasn't taking no shit from him and he needed that. She was witty and quick to say what was on her mind, and the fact that she went to college and obtained a nursing degree made her sexier to him. Her age was a plus cause he wasn't into games and shorty played none, which was a plus for him. He had an agenda and that was to find his queen, and she was the perfect candidate.

After looking at the time, he saw that he had a good 15 minutes before he was due in the chambers, so he decided to scarf down his food real quick. About 5 minutes into his meal, there was a knock at the door. He looked up to see Leno walking in with 2 bottles of water and a lemon.

"Ma nigga, you right on time with them joints," Block said, wiping the excess sauce off his hands to grab a bottle to wash his food down with.

"I figured you was gone need them after this murderous shit that's about to go down," said Leno with a look of glee.

"Hell yeah, but I forgot to tell shorty to give me a drink to go," said Block, looking in his desk drawer for a knife to cut his lemon. A plastic one was all that he could find so that would have to do.

"But yo, I wanted to rap a taste with you about something. After we done with this shit, I'm taking the rest of the day off to chill with Chelle, so I will be off the radar for the rest of the day," said Leno, helping himself to a wing and a seat.

"So, is you asking me or telling me nigga? You act like you a worker or something bruh; you a boss in this shit just like me, nigga. Shit, you don't need my permission," Block said with a laugh.

"I know nigga. I just wanted to let you know; just in case you had some shit planned for later today or something," Leno said as he pulled out his ringing phone. He saw it was a number he didn't recognize, so he silenced it. "I'm trying to chill with shorty and it ain't on no fucking shit either son. I just wanna pick her brain some more; you know, see where her head is at," he said, putting his phone down on the desk.

"I know exactly what you mean, ma nigga. I ran into pink dress at the bar today," Block said, making eye contact.

"Wordddd, but who the fuck is pink dress?" Leno said while laughing.

"Should have known yo drunk ass wouldn't remember. But yo, grab that other bottle and shit for me, son; I'm a finish this shit downstairs. It's about that time," Block said as he grabbed his to-go plate and walked around the desk towards the door.

As they made their way downstairs to the chambers, as they liked to refer it, Block mentally prepared himself for what he was about to do. He said a silent prayer and asked God to forgive him for taking, yet, another life. He knew the act he was about to commit would be heinous; yet, he felt it had to be done, to make a statement and remind niggas of who the boss was.

"Good evening ladies and gentlemen," Block said, walking into the main room where everyone was gathered and patiently waiting. "Keisha baby, what you know," he said, walking over to her, genuinely happy to see her.

"I don't know shit sweetie; what it do," she said, as she reached in for a hug. "He's all set and ready to go," she whispered in his ear, referring to Gutta, the guest of honor.

"Great, thank you, Keish; you the best sweetheart," Block said, turning his attention back to his crew. "Keisha, is everybody accounted for? Are we all here?" he asked, looking around at all the faces of his workers to make sure they all were in attendance and on time. "What about the dues that was owed from last night's extravaganza?"

"Yeah, they straight and we all here, all 30 of us," she said, checking a second time to make sure she was correct.

"Alright, so before we get started, who can tell me what snitching is?" Block asked, as he looked into the crowd of faces. Most of the crew looked on, confused as to why he was asking that.

"Okay, so one. I'm a need one of you niggas to define the word snitch if you will please," he said, taking a seat on the table and biting into a chicken wing.

"A person who tells on somebody!" someone shouted out.

"A dead mutha fucka," another one of them said.

"Bam," Leno said in reference to the remarks being made. He was loving the way Block showed his bossed up side. His swag was on ten and his demeanor was very intimidating.

"Precisely, ladies and gentlemen, a dead mutha fucka who tells on somebody when it's not even necessary," he said, pausing in between the last few words for a dramatic effect. "Do I not pay y'all enough money or something?" he asked, staring at all of their faces while waiting on a response. After not receiving any, he moved on.

"What is the number one rule when being interrogated by the police?" Block asked, wiping his hands after finishing up the last of his meal. "Yo, hand me that water bottle bruh," he said to Leno with an outstretched hand. "Preciate that bruh," he said, grabbing the bottle with lemon that Leno so graciously placed in it. After finishing the bottle off in one long gulp, he started back up with his line of questioning.

"Ahhhhh, that shit hit the spot, ma nigga; we gone need some more of these," he said, tossing the bottle to the floor. "Now, where was I? Oh yeah, the police and what we say during interrogation," Block said, removing a pair of gloves from his pocket and putting them on. "Come on now, don't everybody speak at once, what's up."

"Nothing, you don't say nothing," said Flip, one of his lieutenants.

"Exactly ma nigga, you don't say shit, not a fucking word right," Block said. "And if you get caught up by 12, what do you do?" he asked, making eye contact with a few people while pacing back and forth.

"You ask for a lawyer named Eric Seinfeld and give him the code 492 when he gets there, that way he'll know that you apart of the crew," said Boogie.

"Alrightttt, so if niggas know this, then tell me why we here? I mean, I'm just tryna make sure we all on the same page here. I'm just tryna make sure that we all know that we have rules in place for a reason; we all know that, right. RIGHT!" he said, his voice slightly elevated.

They all shouted different words of acknowledgment and shook their heads up and down, letting him know that they agree.

"Okay, so if you all can be so kind as to follow me this way," he said, using a hand gesture to show which direction he wanted them to go in. "Let us see what's behind door number one," Block said right before opening the door to the torture chambers.

On the other side of the door, Gutta was tied to a chair with a black pillowcase over his face. Leno instructed everyone to make a loose circle around him and the weapons table that was placed in the middle of the floor. Block walked over to the table and grabbed a mini sludge hammer and forcefully removed the cover off his face. Raising his head, Gutta blinked a few times to adjust his eyes to the light. Unable to move a limb, he took a look around as panic began to set in.

"Leno, what's good fam; what's this about?" Gutta asked, his voice quivering.

"You know what this is little nigga, don't play stupid," Leno said as he walked closer to get eye level with him. "I vouched for you, nigga, and you made me look like a fool. What you thought we ain't know, like we wasn't gone find out? We got eyes and ears everywhere nigga; we run this fuckin city. Before you could even finish ya statement, I was made aware of ya snitching status nigga, so ain't no use in playing dumb cause you already know what it is ma nigga," he said through a clenched jaw.

"Man, I was in a tight spot; they had a nigga back against the wall man," Gutta said with present fear, but that didn't stop him from begging for his life in front of all those people.

"Let me stop you right there, little nigga; ain't no sense in trying to explain. Your fate was sealed the minute you opened your mouth to 12," Block said. "Yeaaa, I stayed up late last night thinking of different ways to kill you and what instruments to use. Since I was having such a hard time figuring that out, I thought I would use them all," he said as he walked up to Gutta and placed the sludge hammer in his lap. "Guess we'll start with this then," he said as he turned back to his audience.

"The reason I asked you all here today is to remind you of who you fucking with. I know you might think of me as the laid back type, which I am, but let's be clear. I didn't become a boss by being nice and letting shit slide. I didn't become a boss by playing the background and never getting dirt on my hands; no, my hands are very much dirty, and I'm here today to show you all just how I get down," Block said while making continuous eye contact with the inner circle. He walked around to the back of the chair and placed his hands on his shoulders.

"And, for the record, nigga, these walls are sound proof," Block said with tight lips as he grabbed the sludge hammer, bringing it down on his left knee with full force and shattering his bone on impact.

"Fuuccckkkk!! muthaaa!! Fuucckka!" Gutta yelled out in pain.

"Somebody grab me that duct tape, so I can shut this nigga up," Block said with a menacing look. "Put it over his mouth nigga!" he yelled at Flip. After the tape was placed over his mouth, Block continued with his mission to cause him immense pain.

He walked over to the table to choose his next instrument of pain. Deciding on the wire cutters, he proceeded to cut the tips off of each finger while mumbling incoherently to himself.

"Niggas must think I'm a bitch or some shit, like niggas ain't fearing me in these streets no more. Like y'all must think I'm some fuck boy ass nigga who ain't never put in no work," Block said under his breath as he cut off Gutta's fingertips.

His workers looked on silently in horror, while Leno stood back with a look of pure satisfaction. He didn't know his friend had it in him; to watch somebody, who's normally laid back, torture a person had him at a loss of words.

"Pass me the salt, ma nigga; he bout to wake his bitch ass up," Block said to Leno.

By the time Block got to the third finger, Gutta's body went into shock, causing him to pass out from the severe pain he felt. His words were unheard and muffled by the tape; one could only imagine the pain Gutta truly felt.

Block forcefully placed Gutta's hand into a bowl of salt, causing him to wake up from his pain-induced slumber. Even with the tape covering his mouth, you could still make out the words "fuck" and "shit" through his muffled cries. Block walked over to the table with a twisted smirk on his face, gazing at his new weapon of choice; a sandblaster. Just as Block turned his back, Gutta's body went into convulsions and foam slowly seeped out the sides of the tape. They didn't know it at the moment, but Gutta died from asphyxiation; he choked on his own vomit. The way his body shook so violently, he would have knocked the chair over had it not been bolted to the ground.

"Yo son, that nigga foaming at the mouth!" one of Block's workers yelled.

"Remove the tape nigga!" Block yelled as he ran over to him. He snatched the tape from his mouth and pushed his body as far forward as the rope would allow him to go. The remaining vomit spilled out of his mouth.

"Look at that nigga eyes yo," Duff said to no one in particular. "Them shits is rolled all the way to the back."

Block gave him the look of death, symbolizing *shut up*. He focused his attention back to Gutta; he attempted to stick his finger down his throat, but his tongue was in the way. Seconds later, he stopped shaking and his body slumped forward, just as his last breath left his body.

"Damn, I guess that shit was too much for him son," Leno said, patting Block on the back. "Don't sweat it though; I think niggas got the point," he said.

Block stood there for about 30 seconds, thinking that he wasn't happy with the way things ended. His intentions were to cause a lot more damage than he already did. He took a deep breath before he addressed his crew; he wanted to give them time to process what they just saw.

"Now, do I have everybody's attention?" he asked, as he looked at all the faces in the crowd. Too afraid to utter a word, they all shook their heads in agreeance and remained silent.

"So, going forward, there will be no more issues right?" asked Block. "Do anybody have any questions about how I run my shit? This is an honest question; I really would like to know if y'all have any concerns about how I run ma shit, any at all?" he asked while making eye contact with his workers and waiting on a response. After waiting 30 seconds or so and still receiving silence, he moved on.

"Cool, so that means everybody knows what's expected of them and y'all understand all the rules and regulations set forth," he said while taking off his gloves and grabbing a water bottle of the table. "Get Adrian on the line and let him know it's time," Block said, looking directly at Keisha.

"He gets off in 30 more minutes; he's coming straight over. I'll be happy to wait here with the body until he gets here," Keisha said, speaking up for her man with pride.

"That's a bet; as always, it's a pleasure to see you, sweetie. Call me if you have any issues," he said as he gave her a kiss on the cheek. "Flip and Boogie, y'all stay here with Keisha until A gets here," Block said to his lieutenants.

"As for the rest of y'all, it's back to business as usual," he said, walking towards the stairs. "Oh, one more thing," he said with a pause. "I don't have to tell ya to keep ya mouth shut, do I?" Block asked with a look of death in his eyes.

"Nah fam, what's understood don't have to be explained, right," Flip said, speaking for his comrades. He had seen enough for one day.

"Good, cause everybody claim to be a real nigga until a real nigga walk in the room. I would hate to body anybody else; believe it or not, I got love for each and every one of you in this room. If I didn't trust me, you wouldn't be here," was the last thing Block said before he dipped off into his office.

Him and Leno always kept a change of clothes in the office for situations such as this one. He showered with the special soap Adrian gave him used to remove any and all traces of blood from his skin, rinsed, then dried off. He made up his mind to shower again when he got home; the soap made his skin feel extra dry, due to its special ingredients. He sprayed a few squirts of bond, then put on a new sweat suit and a fresh pair of Timberlands. Grabbing his bloody clothes and shoes, he placed them into a trash bag then tied it up. He grabbed his keys, along with the other contents that was in his pockets, and made his way downstairs. When he opened up the door, Leno was standing in the hallway waiting for him to finish up, so they could talk.

"Damn nigga, how long you been standing there?" asked Block.

"Bout 10 to 15 minutes, just wanted to touch bases with you real quick," Leno said, passing him a bottle of water and lemon slice.

"Swear to God nigga, you be right on time with these joints fam," Block said with a chuckle.

"You already know, ma nigga," was all Leno said.

"So, what's up?" Block said, as he stepped back into the office to take a seat.

"I don't think we'll have any more issue with niggas and they loose lips going forward," Leno said as he closed the door behind him. "Niggas used to ma madness, but I think it shocked them to see that side of you; hell, Mrs. Jenkins looked like she was about to have a heart attack when you started cutting the nigga fingers off, clutching her chest and shit," Leno said with a laugh.

"Mannn shit, I ain't do half the damage I wanted to with the nigga dying on me and shit; I wanted to sandblast his fucking skin off," Block said, staring off in the distance while twisting his fitted cap; clear signs that he was getting angry all over again.

"You did good fam; you made ya point and that's all that matters," Leno said. "But yo how do you wanna handle this Loci and Marlon situation?" he asked as he looked Block in the eye.

"Did you situate the payment with our lawyers?" Block asked, still in deep thought.

"Yeah, I handled that shit yesterday in full, wired straight to they account," Leno said.

"Good, good, give me a few days to think it over; I'm a let him think that shit is sweet before I make my move. Put some eyes on them niggas though, them and Geechee. I wanna dead all them niggas at the same time, ya feel me," Block said as he stood up to leave.

"I'm on it, just let me know when it's time to swoop in and grab em," Leno said with a smirk.

"Bet, I think I might slide out of town for a few days mann; I need a quick little get away to clear ma head, you know," Block said as he checked his phone that chimed, signaling a text message. Smiling to himself, he got silent as he replied, then placed it back into his hooded jacket pocket. "I might even see if lil mama wanna go with me," he said with a genuine smile on his face.

"Not Mr. I don't wine and dine these bitches; plus, you never bring sand to the beach ma nigga," Leno said with an amused look on his face.

"I know son, and normally I'm against all that shit, but it's just something about shorty that makes me want to do that for her, ya know. Like, I feel the need to protect her and be honest with her and shit, and I just met her today ma nigga. It's like, I can feel it in here that she's the one for me," Block said, pointing to his heart. "The shit sound crazy, I know it, but she made a nigga feel comfortable soon as she smiled at me, ma nigga. Do you know she asked me what I did for a living, and I told her the truth without so much as a second guess? It just came right out, like it was nothing major about it," Block said, as if he was replaying the moment right then.

"Damn fam, it's like that," Leno said with a shocked expression. Truth was, he knew exactly how his best friend felt, and since Block was expressing his feelings on ole girl, Leno decided he would come clean about how he felt about Michelle.

"I know, crazy right," Block said as he took a sip of water. "Like, how can I be so sure after one encounter with this woman but, truth be told, ma nigga, I haven't the slightest idea. All I know is my gut is telling me that this is ma queen, and you know I always go with ma gut; hell, it ain't steered me wrong yet. Plus, I've been with enough bitches to know when something has potential, and lil mama definitely has that," Block said, finishing up the last of his bottled water.

"I feel you, ma nigga; I jive feel the same way about Chelle. Shidd, I checked Chu about her ass earlier; I just felt like it wouldn't be right unless I said something to him," Leno said, looking at Block.

Now it was Block's turn to be shocked; he never thought Leno could love a woman other than his aunt, Keisha. It was no secret that Block was looking for his special counterpart to marry and start a family with. But, Leno being interested in just one woman was news to him; he thought it was just the physical attraction with him and Chelle, but now he knew he was mistaken. It was much more than that, if he felt the need to defend her in her absence.

"Worddd," Block said with wide eyes and a look of pure amazement on his face.

"Hell yeah, he was on some disrespectful shit talking about he was looking forward to seeing her fat ass in a tight skirt and shit. For whatever reason, I felt the need to tell him that the topic of her ass was off limits and that she was spoken for," Leno said, surprised at his own honesty. "I just can't stop thinking about her, B; like, as soon as my mind goes blank, my thoughts curve to her. The shit's scary to me, B. I'm not sure what this feeling is but I kinda like it; I just hope ma gut ain't steering me in the wrong direction. And, I'll body that bitch if she ever play me on some on hoe shit," Leno said, scrunching up his face.

"I don't think Chelle's like that; she's one of the good ones dude," Block said.

"Yeah, I know, but you know how I be when it comes to this love shit son, but yo, let me get up out of here, ma nigga. I'm gone take me a nap real quick before I meet up with Chelle later," Leno said, slapping hands with Block.

"That's a bet; I need to give these clothes to Keisha, so Adrian can get rid if these bitches for me," Block said as they walked towards the door. "I'll call you and let you know when I decide where I'm going," he said.

"Alright, get at me a little later," Leno said as he walked in the opposite direction, taking the back steps to his car.

That's one thing Block loved about their friendship; they could discuss anything with each other without any judgment, only honesty. Here it was, he was thinking Leno would look at him crazy for saying the things he was saying about Chasity, and he was experiencing the same exact thing himself. He truly hoped that Michelle was the one for Leno; maybe it would calm him down a bit, help him not be so impulsive, knowing he had a lady at home waiting on him. But, sane or insane, Leno was his right hand man and he loved him regardless.

He heard Adrian's voice as he was coming down the stairs; he walked up to him and gave him a pound just before handing him his bag of soiled clothes.

"What's good, ma nigga; you already know what to do with them joints," Block said, pointing to the bag.

"I got you fam; I got you. But yo, yous a wild dude; Keisha told me you did it in front of the whole crew, even old ass Mrs. Jenkins son. Damn, I hate I missed that shit," he said with a hearty laugh.

"Hell yeah, I had to prove a point ma nigga; they had to know what will happen when you go against the grain in anyway, ya dig. Niggas act like they got amnesia, like they forgot and shit," Block said as he laughed as well. "What better way to prove I'm not having it other than to show them, so they can see it with their own two eyes," he said.

"Right, let me get to it, so I can go home and lay up; I'll make sure to give Keisha ya bill nigga," Adrian said, holding up the bag and laughing still.

"You already know son, fuck with me!" Block yelled as he walked out the door to his car.

He was on the way to use his at-home gym and ponder on a few things. Working out always served as an outlet for Block and so did solitaire. Something about the card game relaxed him; maybe it was the silence mixed with the eye to hand coordination. When stressed, he would work out; when faced with a great adversity, he would play solitary; today, he would do both. The situation with Loci and his association with Geechee had him stressed. He had been caught slipping and, to Block, there was nothing worse than that. On the other hand, he was slightly confused about his take on Chasity. He wasn't sure if he was moving in the right direction when it came to her. On one hand, he was thinking he should go with his gut feeling but, on the other hand, he was unsure if love would come that easy to him. Or was the need to find his queen creating an inter deception, causing him to believe that it was love at first sight. A quick workout, a game of solitare, and a short getaway would clear up any reservations that he might have. He felt that if they got away from the everyday stress of the town and took time to get to know one another, then he would have his confirmation by the time that he returned home.

Making his way into the house, he removed his shoes and went straight to his gym. He decided it would be best to wait until he worked out before he took his second shower; no sense in washing up if he would have to do it again after his workout session. Removing all of his clothes, he went to relieve himself; all the bottles of water he drank earlier had finally caught up with him. After washing his hands, he proceeded to put on his workout gloves and exercise in the nude. Barbells in his hand and balls freely swinging, he did 5 sets of 20, then switched to the treadmill. He loved to workout naked; to him, it was a way for him to become one with his body. He ran the equivalent of 5 miles on the treadmill without so much as one shoe on his foot.

Block took pride in taking care of his body, which was why he drank so many bottles of water each day. He would enjoy a soda with his lunch and dinner but, any other time of the day, he would drink water. He had read somewhere once that a high daily intake of water kept your skin looking healthy and young, as well as naturally flushing out your system. He was all about eating healthy and staying fit; besides smoking weed, he didn't have any bad habits.

After he finished his run, he decided to call it quits for the day; next time, he would focus on just his back. He grabbed his towel and a bottle of water and made his way to the bathroom to shower.

While grooming himself, he thought about the last time he had sex and realized it had been almost a month since his last sexual encounter. Pouring a generous amount of soap in his hand, he began to stroke his member slowly. Back and forth, he stroked with a nice firm grip, stopping to pay special attention to the head every so often. He envisioned it was Chasity's tight warm mouth choking his dick like a pair of vise grips. Juices ran down the sides of her mouth as soft moans escaped her juicy lips. He imagined her picking up speed and swallowing him whole with no gag reflex; it felt like she sucked the soul out of his body. The way that he lathered his lower region, it was sure to get him squeaky clean. Focusing on just the head, he climaxed moments later with thoughts of what her mouth would really do once they took it to that level. It was one of the most powerful nuts that he had ever given himself, and the illusion of her beautiful face was what brought him to it. Block had a feeling that her head game was superb and her pussy was even better. She walked like her shit was gold, and he was in the gold mining business.

Washing the rest of his body, Block rinsed and turned the water off. He grabbed his black fluffy towel and dried his body off.

He pulled a pair of basketball shorts and a wife beater out of the dresser drawer to throw on. On his way to the kitchen, he stopped in the gym room to grab his phone; he noticed the flashing light, indicating he missed calls and messages.

Checking his call log first, he saw one from Chasity and a text from Leno and Adrian, telling him everything was all good at the chambers. He replied with a thumbs up emoji and decided to call Chasity back after his card game.

He needed time to think over the situation and figure out how he would go about asking her on the trip, without him looking crazy. Who would she go out of town with a man she only seen twice? Although the act was spontaneous, it may make him come off as deranged or stalker like. They knew nothing about each other, so he wouldn't be surprised at all if she told him no; hell, he halfway expected it. Block grabbed two bottles of water, some lemon, and two small bags of baby carrots out the refrigerator for a light snack.

He would call his friend, Amir, later to book their hotel and flight, if she decided to come along. Block met Amir when they were in college. Amir went to school for Business management as well, but he was a genius when it came to numbers and making additional profit. Amir was the reason Block owned a staffing agency, a few laundry mats, and a slew of other properties and businesses. He convinced him early on to turn his drug money into taxable money; that way, he would always fly under the federal radar. If Block wanted to, he could have been got out of the game, but it was the power he held that kept him in it, and the fact that he had yet to see a billion dollars cash on his bank statement. Amir was a kid from the streets that made sure he got out as soon as he turned of age. He wanted more out of life and he worked his ass off to get to where he was today. He promised Block that, as long he kept his name clear in the streets, he would help him make a billion dollars by the time he was 30 and, so far, he was keeping up with his end of the bargain.

While playing solitaire, he reflected on everything that happened in the past two weeks, from them killing Jack, Leno killing Tone, to Gutta snitching, and the shootout at the club with Geechee and his crew. Not to mention, the issue of Loci and Marlon stealing his money and work, and the connection Loci had to Geechee. And then there was her; the beautiful and sexy Ms. Chasity, who hadn't left his mind since he first laid eyes on her. There was just something about her that made him want her something awful. He wanted to take her places she never been before. He wanted to show her the side of him that would cherish her and treat her like the queen that she was. He wanted to shield her from all the wrong that the world offered.

Block decided that he would deal with them niggas personally when he came back from his trip this weekend. It would give them a few days to enjoy living cause, little did they know, they'd be dead by the end of the week.

After he completed his game of cards, he elected to call her back to see what's up. She picked up after a few rings; her sweet voice was like music to Block's ears.

"Hello," Chasity said, answering the phone.

"Hey ma, sorry I missed your call; I was working out," he said

"That's okay. I didn't really want anything; I just wanted to ask you about a comment you had made earlier, that's all," she said.

"Oh yea, ask away," Block said as a smile spread across his face. He knew she was talking about his pink dress comment.

"Soooo, how did you know I wore a pink dress yesterday?" she asked with a smile of her own.

"I know about everything worth knowing in ma city baby," Block said for added mystery.

"No, I'm serious Chauncey," Chasity said.

"Cause I saw you; now, let me ask you something," Block said.

"Saw me where though?" she asked, clearly avoiding his question to get her own answered.

"Where did you go when you wore the dress ma?" Block asked, forcing her to answer her own question.

"To, to a club with one of my girlfriends from work," she said, her voice trailing off just as she remembered who he was. He was the fine chocolate specimen that got out the black truck with a cute light skinned guy with long braids.

"Right, I saw you standing in line; truth be told, I watched you all night until that crazy shit popped off," he said with honesty.

"I know I saw you too," she said breathlessly.

"Now, let me ask you something; what would say if I asked you to go out of town with me for a few days?" Block asked, silently holding his breath.

On the other end of the phone, Chasity was silent. She really didn't know how to respond to his question. What was she supposed to say? She knew nothing about this man. She wasn't in the streets like she used to be, but she could find out who he really was if she asked her cousin, Monica. Monica knew everybody whose name made noise in the streets, so if he was out there like he claimed to be, then Monica would know who he was and she would let her know if fucking with him would be a good move or not. But on the other hand, she could use a vacation; she hadn't been anywhere since last year when her and Brook from work went to Miami.

After what felt like 5 minutes of silence, Block cleared his throat and asked was she okay.

"Uh yea, I'm fine; let me call you right back Chauncey," she said right before she disconnected the call.

"What the fuck was that about?" Block said to himself out loud while looking at the phone.

He expected some resistance from her, but he didn't think she would be so short with him. He was prepared to state his case; he practiced what he would say to her if she declined his invitation. But he wasn't prepared for her to hang up on him.

"Damn," Block said out loud as he threw the phone on the couch beside him. "A nigga can't catch a break."

Chasity

Chasity quickly called her cousin Monica right after she got off the phone with Block. As soon as she answered the phone, Chasity went right in with the questions.

"Hey chick, you busy," said Chasity.

"Nah Bitch, you good; what's up," said Monica.

"You ever heard of a dude named Block?" Chasity asked her favorite cousin.

"Have I? What rock you been under bitch? He's only the top nigga in the game right now, him and his right hand Leno. Wit they fine asses, why do you ask?" Monica questioned, smacking loudly on her gum.

"Cause Block asked me to go out with him; I just needed some background on him, that's all," Chasity said.

"Okay bitch, go; hell, if you don't, I will. Do you know how many hoes be at him and get nowhere?" Monica asked, all dramatic. "Like, for real Chas, these bitches be throwing all kinds of pussy at him and he don't even budge. If this nigga actually asked you out on some date type shit, then trust me, it's worth it. His name may be out there, but it's on some get money shit, not no friendly nigga shit, ya feel me," she said with a pause, like she was waiting on Chasity to respond.

"So, he really the man around here hun? And he ain't just hoeing around is what you saying?" she asked for confirmation.

"Put it this way bitch, I don't know not one female in these streets that can say they been with him, and you know that I know everybody," Monica said as she paused between words to show how serious she was.

"Okay, thanks chick; alright, I gotta go. I'll call you back later on, love you, BYE," Chasity said as she hung up on yet another person in less than 10 minutes.

After talking to her cousin, Chasity sat there and weighed her options for a few minutes. She didn't get a bad vibe from him when they talked earlier, and she usually was a good judge of character. When he felt like he had offended her this afternoon, he apologized and asked to start over and, to her, that showed he had integrity. Plus, he was completely honest with her when asked what he did for a living and he said sell drugs. She appreciated his truthful nature; it was definitely welcomed and refreshing, considering the breed of niggas buffalo had to offer at the present time. Even the corporate niggas were full of shit; hiding wives and side pieces, only to add another chick to their roster. Then there was the reaction she felt to his touch; it had been a while since she felt something so powerful from a man's touch. Last time she felt anything remotely close to it was with her ex-boyfriend Geechee, but that was nearly eight years ago. She broke it off with him when she found out he was arrested for rape; she refused to stay with a man who felt the need to cheat and forcefully take the pussy, for that matter.

She was coming up on her four-day rotation, meaning she would be off for four days in a row, so he actually caught her at the right time. She decided to live a little and take him up on his offer; she would call him back in 30 minutes. It was nearly 7:00 and her shift was almost over. Chasity had to make her last rounds to check on her patients and sign off on their charts.

Block

Block looked at the ringing phone and wondered if he should answer it or let it go to voicemail. He wasn't too fond of being hung up on, without so much as a goodbye or an explanation as to why. He went to answer the phone just as it stopped ringing. He was just about to call her back when she called again; he answered immediately this time.

"Hello," Block said, his voice full of irritation.

"I'm sorry, was I interrupting anything?" Chasity asked, catching onto the sound of his voice.

"Nah ma, you good, what's up," he said, softening his voice a little.

"Oh okay, well is the offer still on the table?" she asked, getting straight to the reason for her call.

"It sure is, what made you change your mind?" asked Block.

"I never gave you an answer, just like I'm not now. I simply asked a question," Chasity said.

"Touché sweetheart, touché" Block said with a smirk on his face.

"But I would love to accompany you on your trip out of town; this isn't one of the special trips, is it?" Chasity asked, referring to a dope run.

"Of course not, I'm not in the business of putting anyone's life in jeopardy, especially unknowingly," Block said, slightly offended. "Trust me ma, you will know all the risks there is to know about if you fucking with me, ya dig."

"I understand; I just had to ask," Chasity said as she shrugged her shoulders like Kanye.

"That's respect sweetheart; no hard feelings, so where would you like to go? I was thinking some place warm, like Florida," Block said, quickly changing the subject.

"Florida's okay, but I went to Miami last year; how about Hawaii or someplace tropical," she said, testing the waters a bit.

"Hawaii's fine, as long as you can get the time off of work," he said, surprised at his own answer. He was thinking of leaving stateside, but he did ask her to choose.

"Well, I have four days off; that should be enough time, shouldn't it?" asked Chasity.

"Well, considering it's a 12-15-hour flight both ways, then you have to factor in the fact that we would have to leave the morning of day three, just to get you home in time for work, it's possible," Block said with a slight chuckle.

"Touché sir, Florida it is," she said with a laugh.

"That's more like it and it will only take two and a half hours approximately," he said. "But I will take you to Hawaii if you really wanna go," Block said in a serious tone.

"No, we'll save that for another time; when should I be ready?" asked Chasity.

"Now would be good; I'll call my travel agent as soon as we get off the phone, then I can pick you up at your house on the way to the airport," said Block.

"No, I'll meet you at yours; if I'm going out of town with a stranger, I need to know where to have my mother send the police, just in case I don't make it back home," she said on a more serious note.

Block sat there quietly thinking about her request; he wasn't cool with people knowing where he laid his head. But seeing as though she was taking a chance on him, he would do the same.

"You must don't trust your future too much," Block said with a chuckle.

"Well, seeing as how uncertain one's future can really be, I feel the need to tread lightly, since I'm still unsure of what lies ahead for me and my said future," Chasity said, feeling good about her response.

"Damn, it's like that ma," Block said, clutching his chest like it hurt, as if she could see it.

"It most definitely is," she said in a matter of fact like tone.

"Well, alright then, but you gone make me do something to you with that mouth of yours ma," he said with a hint of seduction in his voice.

Chasity sat silent for a few seconds with her voice caught in her throat. "Umm, so are you okay with my terms sir?" she asked with a firm voice.

"That's cool, but if you can please instruct your mother to not give my address out to anyone until after whatever deadline you set for her to hear from you has passed. Nobody knows where I lay my head and I would like to keep it that way," Block said in the most pleasant but firm voice he could muster up.

"Of course, I'll be sure to let her know," Chasity said, happy that he obliged her request. Little did Block know, if he would have said no, then she wouldn't have gone.

"Now that we got that out the way, how long will you keep your future waiting sweetheart," he said in a more playful tone.

"Not very long, give me an hour to take off this monkey suit and get cleaned up. I will text you when I'm on my way," she said as she was pulling into her driveway.

"Alright sweetheart, see you in a minute and pack light if you can, okay," he said as he walked in his bedroom to tidy up a bit.

"Okay, see you soon, bye," Chasity said, removing the phone from her ear as she hung it up.

Block shot Amir a quick text, telling him to book him a private flight for two, with a two bedroom, two full bathroom villa on beachfront property leaving asap. He texted back 15 minutes later with the itinerary set to leave at 10:00 tonight. He sent him a thumbs up text and proceeded to get ready; the hardest part was getting her to agree, but that was now over.

Leno

After leaving the chambers, Leno went home to freshen up and change clothes really quick, then he made his way to Michelle's house to take her out for dinner. He decided to go grown man style and wear a button down shirt, blue jeans, and a pair of classic wheat Timberlands. He wasn't sure where she wanted to eat, so he would play it safe and dress for anything.

He was surprised at the extra effort he was putting in for Michelle. Normally, he wouldn't dare go out his way to take a woman out in public, let alone dress to impress her. He even wore a Gucci scarf and hat to accessorize with it, followed by Gucci by Gucci cologne. He was looking good and smelling good; he was confident that she would approve of his efforts tonight. Pulling up to the address she gave him, he parked and got out to knock on the front door, another first for him; normally, he would he just beep the horn for them to come outside.

Michelle answered the door in a pantsuit with no shirt underneath; her breasts were strategically placed front and center, as if she had tape holding them up. Leno licked his lips as he closed the door behind.

"Hi, come on in and make yourself at home hun. I'll just be a few more minutes," Michelle said as she walked to the back of the house.

Leno decided to have a look around the living room while he waited for her to finish up. He walked over to the fireplace and looked at the pictures that were on the mantle. There were a few of her and Keisha at various locations, and one of an older women and man he assumed to be her parents. She kept a clean and cozy home that smelled of apple pie and other various fruits, which was a must for him. He looked around for a few more minutes before she emerged from the back area looking like a tall glass of chocolate milk to him.

Realizing he was indeed staring longer than necessary, he cleared his throat and asked was she ready to go. She shook her head yes and grabbed her coat and purse off the table by the door on their way out. Little did he know, she was in fact staring as well, and she was taking inventory of the things she noticed that were different about him. Gone were the sneakers and flashy name brand clothing; this look had him looking less like a thug and more like a man. Truthfully speaking, it had her speechless and nervous at the same time; nevertheless, she definitely liked what she saw.

Leno waited by the steps while she locked the front door, then opened the door for her and helped her get in the truck. Once she was secure and in the vehicle, he walked to his side and got in. Starting the car up and pulling off, he started by asking her if she was okay with Italian food. She said she was, so he proceeded to drive to Salvatore's, one of the most popular Italian restaurants in the city. They made small talk about this and that to help the time pass on the drive over. He glanced at her ever so often, in awe at how amazing she looked to him. That pantsuit was hugging her curves in all the right places, and her titties was sitting pretty in her chocolate colored blazer that complemented her bronze like skin. No longer able to take the on and off silence, he turned his Pandora app to Future and Dej Loaf's *Hey There*.

"Okayyy, this my shit," Michelle said while twerking in her seat.

"Damn ma, it's like that," Leno said with a laugh.

"I love me some Future hunni," she said, slow twerking and snapping her fingers.

"Okay, so all I gotta do is play some Future and you'll bust it open for a real nigga," he said, keeping his eyes on the road. He looked over at her and the face she held made him wished he wouldn't have said that, but her mouth said something different.

"I don't need Future to do that sweetheart," she said with a sexy smirk in her face and went back to twerking.

"Damn, you had a nigga ready to stop at the nearest flower shop and shit," he said with a chuckle and holding his chest, as if his heart really hurt.

"Don't let me stop you," Michelle said with a serious look on her face.

"Say no more ma," Leno said as he googled flower shops near his current location. He honestly had no idea where one was; he never had use for one until now. Keisha always put fresh flowers on his mother, Trudy's, grave for both of them.

There was one 5 miles back in the opposite direction on Genesee St. and Olcott Pl. called Eckel Florist. He made an illegal u-turn to head over to the floral shop. Just as soon as he straightened out his car, an unmarked police car hit their lights, signaling him to pull over. Leno pulled over to the side of the road and killed the engine. He looked at Michelle and told her to be cool that he was clean; no dope was in the car.

"Oh shit, I almost forgot; put this in the glove box," he said, handing her the 9mm pistol that he had on his hip.

"Nah boo, they might check in there; I got it," she said, putting the gun in her purse. "They can't search me; I'm a passenger."

He smiled at her in a proud way; he liked that she didn't hesitate to put the gun in her purse, all signs of a ride or die in his book. She was already aware of who he was and what he did for a living, so it was easier for him to let his hair down around her. His thought was interrupted by a tap on his window. He turned his attention to the officer and imagine his surprise when he saw Detective Jackowski; the cop that robbed him and Block of a million dollars and 20 bricks.

"And how may I help you today officer?" Leno asked through gritted teeth.

"It's Detective, and are you aware that you made an illegal u-turn by an intersection sir?" asked Detective Jackowski with a sly grin on his face.

"No sir, I was not; I also wasn't aware that the great citizens of Buffalo were paying detectives to do minor traffic stops," Leno said with a grin of his own.

"License and registration sir," said Detective Jackowski, already tired of playing the cat and mouse game. He noticed Leno's truck a few blocks back and he was hoping that he did something to warrant him to be pulled over. He was hoping that he would spot paraphernalia in the vehicle or smell marijuana coming from it but, so far, all he had to go on was an illegal u-turn. He despised him and Block just the same, but they seemed to be untouchable these days. "Sit tight while I go and run these," he said before he walked to his car. Now that he had his full name, he was hoping that a warrant would pop up or anything that he could use to remove him from the car to search the vehicle.

"Sure thing Dick-tec-tive," Leno said with a laugh as he walked away.

"What's his problem?" Michelle asked while pointing in his direction.

"He got it out for the kid, but we always come up clean," Leno said, referring to Block and himself.

"Yeah, I kinda figured that much," she said as she sat back in her seat with her hands crossed. Now that she knew this was a bogus stop, she was ready to pop off on the cop. She had been checking for Leno for a long time and she would be damned if she lost her chance over a jealous ass cop and his bogus traffic stops. She decided to call her cousin Devin. Devin was the mayor of Buffalo and he could surely get his ass in line, if no one else could. "What's his name baby?" she asked as she typed away on her keyboard.

"Detective Jackowski, why?" asked Leno with a perplexed look on his face.

"Just wait," she said, pressing send on her phone. Once the line was connected, she went right in in her conversation.

"Hey cousin, how are you? Listen, I'm with my dude and this detective Jackowski pulled us over under false pretenses and he won't allow us to leave. Yes, Jacob Jackowski I presume, in an unmarked car and plain clothes, unless there is another," she said with a wide grin. He assured her he would get right on it and invited her over for dinner to catch up. She accepted his invitation for later next week, then they disconnected the call.

"Just sit tight baby," she said, placing her hands behind her head and lying on them.

"What you got going on ma? Who was that you were talking to?" Leno asked with a confused look.

"Just relax baby, mama got us," she said with a wink.

Out his side mirror, he saw Jackowski walking back towards the driver side door, only to be interrupted by his car radio requesting an immediate response. He looked at her with wide eyes, then back at his mirrors, only to see an upset Detective Jackowski throw his police issued radio back in the car. He'd just received a call from captain John to leave them alone and return to the station immediately. He walked back to the driver's side window with a clear and present scowl on his face to give Leno back his license and registration. But, not before he said what he felt he needed to say.

"Here you are sir," Jackowski said, handing him back his credentials. "Not sure who you know, but I'm sure I'll see you around when the time is right."

"Is that a threat Detective?" Michelle asked as she leaned forward in her seat, now feeling the need to make her presence known.

"Certainly not ma'am, y'all have a great night. You all look very dapper this evening, might I add," he said with a wicked grin.

They both watched on as he walked back to his vehicle; he may have had a smile on his face, but he surely had a look of defeat in his eyes. Leno was sure this wouldn't be his last encounter with dicktective Jackowski, as he called him. He knew that the detective didn't care for him and Block, but he thought it was over when they spared the detective's life months prior to this incident. He also knew that if he had it out for him, then he needed to be extra careful, now that he was in the detective's line of sight.

Once he pulled off, he started in with his questioning, still headed in the direction of the flower shop.

"Who did you call back there, baby girl?" Leno asked, looking between her and the road.

"My cousin Devin, he's the mayor," she said as she removed the gun from her purse to give back to him.

"Thank you," he said, reaching for the weapon and securing it back on his hip. "I didn't know you were related to the mayor of Buffalo; why didn't you tell me?"

"Hell, you never asked," said Michelle with a laugh.

"True," said Leno with a laugh. "Thank you for that though; I really appreciate it ma. Thanks for everything," he said as he licked his lips.

He was approaching a red light when he got the sudden urge to feel her lips. Coming to a complete stop, he leaned over in his seat and gently grabbed her face and covered her lips with his. Not really much of a kisser, he did what he felt was right, parting his lips just enough for her to slide her tongue in to play with his. Apparently he was doing something right, cause her breath was caught in her throat and her chest was heaving up and down with her eyes closed. It took for the car behind them to interrupt their lip-locking session; he smiled at her and she started laughing.

"What's so funny ma?" asked Leno, as he tried his best to focus on the road ahead.

"Nothing," Michelle said, smiling to herself.

"You sure it's nothing? This nothing got you laughing hard as hell," he said as he looked back and forth between her and the road.

"It's just that, when you first kissed me, I could tell you're not experienced in that area. I think it's cute though," Michelle said as she bit her bottom lip.

145

"Oh yeah," he said while he licked his lips. "You're right though; I haven't kissed many women; shit's too personal. Your next thought should be why did I decide to kiss you though," he said as he pulled over to the curb in front of the shop.

"I'll be right back ma," he said as he unbuckled his seat belt to quickly get out the car.

"Okay daddy," she said with a sexy smirk.

He turned and looked at her, then winked his eye. "Yeah aight, I see you like to play," he said with a smile, and she busted out laughing.

"Excuse me ma'am, is this your shop?" he asked to the older woman trying her best to get a heavy box in the car. "Let me help you with that ma'am," Leno said, shocking himself; he was never this helpful.

"Thank you, young man; yes, it is but, unfortunately, we're closed for the day," she said, handing him the heavy box to put in the back seat.

"Yes ma'am, I understand, but if you were to open back up for five minutes, I promise I will buy every rose you have in your store," he said, holding up a wad of cash with pleading eyes. He still couldn't believe the extent he was going just to impress her. But the thing she did for him back there a little while ago with Jackowski was enough to let him know she deserved it and more.

The older lady stood there for a moment and thought about it, and although she was very tired, she knew this would be a great payout.

"I don't mean to offend you in anyway, but how do I know you won't rob me when we get in there?"

"I'll tell you what, sweetheart; you hold onto this and, if you owe me any change, you can give it back after we've completed our transaction. How does that sound?" he asked, holding the wad of cash out to her.

After a few seconds, she decided that if he trusted her to hold onto his money, that maybe she should trust him too, and he did help her with her box.

"Come on in son, that's alright, I trust ya, but let me call my husband, Gerald. If I don't show up in the next 15 minutes, he'll start blowing my cellular phone up," she said with a laugh as she walked to the front door of the shop.

"Thank you so much ma'am. I really do appreciate this," he said, meaning every word.

"She must be some kind of lady for you to go through all this trouble," she said as she turned to look him in the eyes.

He took the time to think about what she said, then shook his head and said, "I think so too; she deserves this and much more."

"Well, in that case, let's make this wonderful lady smile a smile so bright, it will light up the whole eastern sea board," she said as she unlocked the door, then rushed to deactivate the alarm. "Give me one minute to call my husband, young man; I'm sorry, what was your name?" she asked.

"Leonardo ma'am," he said, surprised that he gave her his real name.

"Okay Leonardo, give me just a minute; I'm Marjorie by the way. Nice to meet you," she said as she searched her coat pocket for her phone.

"Yes ma'am, likewise," Leno said, deciding that he would have a look around while he waited for her to finish up her call.

After a minute or so, she told him she was good and ready to get started. 30 minutes, 25 dozen, an assortment of 300 long stem roses and 1000 dollars later, he was ready to go. She decided to put two dozen roses to every vase.

"Do you need me to help you get some of these vases to the car? As a matter of fact, you will need a box cause, if not, they will get damaged on the drive to wherever you're going," Mrs. Marjorie said as she walked around the counter to get a few boxes. "It will only take a minute or two to put the vases in the box, two to a box should be about 12 boxes; you will have to carry the last one," she said as she grabbed a vase to put in box. "How about I pack and you take them to the car?" she asked with a warm smile.

"That sounds like a plan," Leno said, returning her a smile. "I'll take the single vase with the dozen in it first," he said as his excitement increased. He took one rose and placed it in his mouth, like he seen it done in movies.

"Okay hun," she said as she looked up for a second.

Leno walked out to the car with one rose in his mouth and a vase behind his back. Michelle looked up from her phone and smiled.

"Took you long enough; I'm starving," she said, opening her door with a laugh. "Thank you, sweetie; how romantic of you," she said, referring to the rose that he had in his mouth. She closed her eyes and inhaled the fresh flowers scent. "I just love flowers; I think all women do."

"Can you hold this for me, ma?" he asked, handing her the vase to walk back into the store.

He went inside and grabbed two boxes at one time to take to the car. Mrs. Marjorie told him to be careful with the boxes and to hold them close to his chest. He politely smiled at her and proceeded out the door, headed for the back seat.

"Unlock the door for me, baby girl," he said as he got closer to the car; she turned around in her seat to unlock the door for him. He used his feet to kick it open the rest of the way. He then went back inside for the two more; he repeated the process until all the boxes were in the car. He then waited for Mrs. Marjorie to lock up and was safely in her car before he got in his to leave.

"What's all this?" Michelle asked, as soon as he got in.

"Flowers," he said, pulling away from the curb, waiting until it was clear to make a u-turn.

"Clearly, but my question is did you buy the whole flower shop Leno?" she asked with a laugh.

"Almost," he said with a wink, as he drove in route to their destination.

"You are something else; I had no idea you were this sweet," she said as she smiled at him.

"Neither did I," he said with a serious face. "But, you make a nigga wanna try," he said, stunned at his own honesty. He was slowly changing into a different man in her presence, a more respectable man, a more thoughtful man. He found himself unable to hide his true feelings and thoughts when he was with her. The more time he spent with her, the more irrelevant Keisha's feeling would become. He couldn't understand how his feelings were so strong in such a short amount of time. True, indeed, he'd known her for some years, but he didn't know her on a personal level. Yet, here he was, stepping outside his comfort zone for her, but it felt so right to him. Like it came naturally to him, almost like second nature.

Pulling up at the restaurant 15 minutes later, Leno parked and got out the car. He went around to Michelle's side of the car to open the door for her. She thanked him with a smile and a gentle, yet passionate kiss, lasting all of 5 seconds. When their lips separated, Leno took a second to admire her beauty close up and personal.

"Thank you," Michelle said breathlessly.

"For what ma?" he asked, still holding her close as he looked into her almond shaped eyes.

"For the flowers and being a gentleman; I know this is all new to you," she said, putting her head down, no longer able to stare into his beautiful grey-blue eyes.

"It is, but I like it," he said as he gently pulled her head up by her chin. "You don't have to thank me, ma; you deserve it and so much more. You also deserve a decent meal on me; let's go eat, a nigga starving," he said with a laugh as he released her from his embrace.

"Leave it to you to ruin a romantic moment; boy, let's go eat," she said, as she playfully slapped him on the arm and laughed.

Two appetizers, two entrees, and five drinks later, they were in the car headed back to her house. Their conversation over dinner and on the ride home was far more in depth, filled with talks of dreams and ambitions, along with long term goals, past relationships, and likes and dislikes. Leno found out that Michelle was an only child and that her first cousins were more like her brothers and sisters. She had only been in 2 serious relationships her whole life and each of them lasted at least 5 years. She loved the 3 F's; food, flowers, and Future. He told her that he was also an only child with no first cousins that he knew about. He told her that his aunt Keisha had been his guardian since the age of 14 and that both of his parents were dead. All of which she already knew, seeing as though her and Keisha had been friends for over 10 years.

Once Leno pulled up to the house, he turned the car off and sat there for a few minutes, not wanting the night to be over. He really had enjoyed her company and wasn't ready for them to depart ways for the evening. As he sat there and admired her beauty, he remembered that he was supposed to text Block and let him know when the Gutta situation was handled. Through the powers that be, his phone hadn't rung at all during their date. He asked her to give him a second to make a call, so he called Adrian to see if everything was all good on his end. Adrian confirmed that it was and that he already texted Block to let him know. He decided to text Block and let him know as well, just so he was double covered, since Block always stressed business before pleasure. Once he was done, he turned his focus back to the beautiful sight before him.

"I enjoyed you today ma," he said as he looked her directly in the eye.

"Likewise sweetie, I did to," she said with a smile.

"I guess you gon need my help getting all these flowers in the house hun?" he said with a chuckle.

"Would you please," she stated, playfully rolling her eyes.

"Say no more baby," said Leno, as he licked his bottom lip. He got out the car to go and open her side of the door, as he had been doing all evening. He then unlocked the trunk and grabbed the first two of the twelve boxes, then she grabbed on as well.

"Go head girl with yo cock diesel ass," he said, laughing at his own joke.

"Ha, ha, ha, whatever nigga," she said as she carefully walked up the steps and placed the box on the floor by the door.

"I love that about you, ma; you're classy and hood, definitely something I could appreciate," he said as he admired her plump backside.

"Leave it to you to give a girl a ratchet ass compliment," she said, smiling while she unlocked the front door. "You can put them on the dining room table Leno," she said as she held the door open for him. Picking up her box, she took hers in the house as well; as soon as he saw her enter with the box, he took the box from her and put it on the table as well.

After three more trips, all the boxes were in the house including the vase he had given her; she opted to place them on the kitchen table.

"I'll be right back sweetie; let me use the restroom and change into my house clothes," she said as she vanished toward the back of the house.

"See what I mean, who the fuck says restroom!" he yelled, so she could hear him.

"Boy shut up," she said, peeking her head out of a door in the back of the house.

While she did her business, Leno decided to take all the vases from the boxes and set them up on the dining room table. She entered the room just as he was on the last box, which held a few packets of powder to make the flowers last longer, a heart shaped balloon, and a card.

"What's all this," she said in awe. It's one thing to know that he bought her a bunch of flowers, but to actually see them was a different story. Their colors varied from white, pink, yellow, orange, purple, and of course, red.

"These are for you, ma," he said with a smile as big as hers.

"And this," she said, pointing to the balloon and card on the table.

"That wasn't me, that was Mrs. Marjorie's doing; hell, open it. I wanna know what it says too," Leno said as he reached for the card.

"Boy move," she said, slapping his hand away as she ripped the envelope open and it read:

A man that is willing to make memories with you

is a man that is willing to move mountains for you

A man willing to show his affection for you

is a man you need to show appreciation to

Accept the good with the bad, and remain in god's light

for a man willing to protect what's his, is a man worth a million prayers.

P.S. I hope his gesture makes your smile light up the whole eastern seaboard.

Signed Marjorie Majors

Michelle looked up from her card with a faint smile and tears in her eyes. Without even second guessing, Leno snatched the card from her hand to see what would make her cry. He quickly scanned over the card and busted out laughing once he got to the end.

"You're such a girl," he said as he pulled her in for a hug.

"Whattt, that was sweet and thoughtful of her," she said with a smile as she wiped her tears.

"Had me thinking it was a death threat or some shit," he said.

"Yeah, the way you snatched that paper from my hand, I almost did," she said with a laugh of her own.

"I just wanted to see what it was that had you crying and shit, that's all," he said as he playfully pushed her arm.

"I thought you was about to pull out a piece and bust a cap in that paper's ass." Michelle laughed as she demonstrated him shooting a gun.

"I see you got jokes, hun? But, fa real, I don't like to see you cry, even if it's a happy cry," he said, getting serious.

"Awww, you fucks with the kid hun?" she asked, as she stood on the tips of her toes to get face to face with him.

"Yeaaa, I fucks with ya clachet ass, that's classy and ratchet all in one," he said with a smile as he moved in for a kiss.

Hugging and kissing each other for a few minutes, Leno excused himself and asked to use her bathroom. She told him it was the first door on the right, off the kitchen hallway. Once inside, he had to adjust himself; he had no idea that kissing could have his member that hard. He splashed some water on his face, flushed the toilet, and washed his hands before going back out there. For the first time in his life, sex was the furthest thing from his mind; he really did like spending time with her and he didn't want to ruin it, assuming she would let him hit.

"Damn, I thought you fell in nigga," she said with a laugh when she spotted him coming from the bathroom.

"Naw, I'm good ma, what else you got going on tonight?" he asked, hoping that she didn't have anything else planned.

"Nothing much but, if you need to leave, I understand," she said; the disappointment present in her voice.

"I'm good, what you got good to watch on DVD; I can't remember the last time I've actually sat down to watch anything," he said

"I got Netflix, we can chill if you want," she said with a slight hesitation. She didn't want to sound desperate, but it had been over a year since she had a man in her house, let alone her bed. And she was way pass due for a freak session. Michelle had no shame; she had known him long enough, she wanted her rocks dusted off, and she knew he would be the right one to do it. She wanted some of that thug passion that 2pac used to talk about in his songs, some straight fucking like the movie Baby Boy type action. Some squeezing, holding, biting, scratching, spanking, screaming, hair pulling action tonight. If he didn't respect her in the morning, she could live with it, but that was a risk she was willing to take. She wanted more from Leno somewhere in the near future but, at the moment, she needed to be sexed something serious.

"Oh word," Leno said with a sexy smirk on his face. He knew what that meant, more like the TV would be watching them. He was all for giving her that thug loving. But he had to let her know up front that, if she gave herself to him in that way, she could never give it to another, not with the feelings that he had growing for her. Leno could be a patient man when necessary, especially if it was something he really wanted. If she had a problem with those terms, then he would either wait or move on. He wasn't hurting for no pussy; he also had walked away from a guaranteed nut for less. So, the choice was hers. He couldn't take it serious if he knew she was out here entertaining other niggas.

"What do you want to watch?" Michelle asked, as she grabbed the remote off the end table to get comfortable on the couch.

"It don't matter ma; I'm down for the Netflix and chill, anything except romance though," he said, pulling her closer to him with her back against his chest.

"Okay, how about Streets? It's about a musically talented young woman who hangs out with some hood niggas, and she gets caught up in a murder investigated by her mother, the new district attorney. It shouldn't be too bad; Meek Mills is starring in it," she said, pressing play as she got comfortable.

"Yeah, he straight," Leno said as he leaned forward to remove the gun from his waist.

Twenty minutes into the movie, Michelle was no longer able to contain herself; she had a desire to feel him inside her and she was ready now. She was sure that he would make the first move, especially with him initiating the first kiss when they were in the car earlier. She knew he was attracted to her; she just figured he was trying to be a gentleman and not take it there with her so soon. But, she had other plans. Michelle turned around on the couch; they were now facing each other chest to chest. She looked into his eyes with lust and hunger as she kissed him passionately. Leno welcomed her advance and returned the passion as he slid his hands down her plump backside. They kissed and touched each other with so much hunger; you would have thought they'd both been sexually deprived for 5 years or more. Michelle removed her shirt as she straddled his lap, putting her pussy on his dick and grinding like a high school student. The friction from her pants and his hardening wood was driving Michelle crazy. The serious lip locking game they were playing didn't make it any better; she had to have it. She stood up to remove her remaining articles of clothing, so they could finally get to it. Just as she got her pants slightly below her ass, Leno stopped her.

"Hold up ma; I can't let you do this," he said, slightly out of breath. His chest heaved up and down from the intense kissing session.

"Hun? What do you mean you can't let me do this?" Michelle asked with present disappointment in her voice.

"I just saying ma; I'm really feeling you and I don't want you to think that's all I want from you cause it's not. I want it be the right time when it happens, and now ain't the time ma."

"Ohhh, alright then," Michelle said as she rushed to put her clothes back on, slightly embarrassed. She had never been rejected before and it kinda hurt her ego.

"Slow down and look at me for a second, baby girl," he said, touching her arm gently. "When that time comes, I want you to give me all of you. And, by that, I mean you can never give it to another, so I want to give you time to make sure that this is what you want," he said while pointing to himself.

"Do you give this option to all the women you sleep with?" she said, sexually frustrated and slightly aggravated.

"No, just one, you ma," he said as he looked her directly in the eye. "You are the first woman that I ever took seriously; I just want things to go the way they are supposed to go naturally. That day will come and when it does, trust me ma, you won't be ready for it."

She looked into his eyes and saw how serious and sincere he was, and she relaxed a little. He truly was being a gentleman, not the thug she heard so much about, but a man that nobody else had ever witnessed. "Okay bae, you right; we'll wait," she said as she stood on her tiptoes to give him a kiss.

"Good, I'm not saying I wasn't gone respect you in the morning, but I probably wouldn't have respected you in the morning," he said while laughing.

"Anndd there goes your ratchet side," she said as she joined in on the laughter. "Well, come on, let's finish with this movie then," she said, pulling him down on the couch with her. As soon as they got good and comfortable, Leno's phone rang. It was Block, who called to say that him and Chasity would be MIA until Tuesday and to look out for the business for him. MIA was code for Miami Florida; they had ways to say enough with saying too much over the phone. He assured his friend that everything would be fine and that he would call him if he needed him, before disconnecting the call. Leno and Michelle resumed watching their movie; by the end of the movie, they both were sleeping peacefully in each other's arms.

Block

He moved around his penthouse quickly, making sure everything was in order before his guest arrived. Chasity called a little while ago, wanting the address so she could be on her way. He instructed her to call once she got to the parking garage, so he could walk her up. He also called down to security to let them know he was expecting a guest and that he would meet them down there once she arrived. Block was fairly nervous; it was the first time that he had anyone over besides Leno and Keisha. His own mother hadn't been over to his house before; he was anxious to know what she thought of his decorating skills. The tastefulness of the design gave off the vibe that a woman may have decorated his place, but that was far from the truth. Block picked out all his own paintings, his own tile, and counter tops; he got it all, even down to the silverware. He raced over to his ringing phone just in time to miss the call. He called right back and told her that he was on the way down. He looked himself over in the hallway mirror, noticing he still had on his basketball shorts and tee shirt. It was too late to change now; he decided he would do that when he got back in. He grabbed his keys with his phone in tow and made his way down in the elevator. Once he reached the bottom level, he waved at old man Joe the security guard on duty for the night, then told her to park her car next to the car with the tarp on it. Block met her at the car and told her to pop the trunk, so he could get her bags to put in his truck.

"How you doing ma? Glad to see you packed light." He laughed in reference to 2 carry-ons and 1 rolling suitcase.

"What? A girl's gotta have options," she said with a smile as she got out the car.

"I told you to pack light for a reason beautiful. Matter of fact, we taking these upstairs and you gon have to filter some of this shit out," he said laughing, as he grabbed the bags and closed the trunk.

"Noooo, I need everything that's in there," she said, pouting and pointing at her bags.

"No you don't, beautiful; I got you, trust me," he said, walking towards the elevator.

"Yeah, you asking me to put a whole lot of faith in a man I know nothing about," she said as she looked down at the ground.

Block looked back at her and studied her for a second; her posture and body language changed the minute the statement came out her mouth. Gone was her confidence and strong will that he was attracted to when he encountered her. In her place stood an unsure woman who lacked self-assurance and confidence; hence her ability to lower her head to the ground when there was no need to. Block was a different breed of man; he believed in watching people closely, looking for lying eyes and questionable body language, mixed with discernment; his ability to read people was unteachable.

He placed her bags down at his feet and walked back over to her; he gently guided her head back up to its rightful resting place. He looked into her eyes for a brief moment before he spoke, "Don't ever allow a man nor woman to remove your self-assurance and confidence ma, even if it's me. You are far too beautiful to be looking at the ground; a queen such as yourself should never look down. If, at any moment, I make you feel the need to drop ya head, then you need not be around me. Do you really believe in you heart that I would harm you in any way? Now, before you answer that question, take a moment to silence you heart and mind. Because before I bring you into my sanctuary, you must know the answer to this question. I refuse to be around a person that I do not trust or one that does not trust me. I know that we just met, but I trust my gut at all times sweetheart, and my gut tells me that you are the one for me. I am a man of very few interests, believe it or not, so if I take interest in something or someone; trust me, it is for good reason. I will allow you a few moments alone to think over what I said, and I'll be right over there waiting when you need me beautiful," said Block with a simple kiss to her forehead before he walked back over to the elevator.

Chasity stood there for a few minutes and thought about what he said. She asked herself the million-dollar question; why was she here? She knew nothing about this man, other than his name, where he lived, and what he did for a living. Him being a drug dealer didn't matter to her; her last boyfriend was a drug dealer and she had plenty others that had the same occupation, so that wasn't an issue. But she was firm believer of trusting her gut feeling as well, and she didn't feel like he would bring her any harm. But you could never be too sure these days. Nevertheless, she decided to go with her gut and take a chance; his demeanor was calming and his words made her feel like she could conquer the world. Any man that would try to convince a woman to see the worth within herself is a man worth trusting, in her eyes. She turned around and smiled at him; when she was close enough, she reached out to grab a hold of his hand. She then reached down to pull the handle up on her roll-on suitcase.

"Lead the way future," she said with a genuine smile. He smiled back and grabbed the rest of her luggage, then pressed the up button on the elevator panel. Once the elevator arrived, they stepped in hand and hand; both were ready to start their new adventure. Block was the first one to break the silence on the way up.

"I never did ask if you had a man beautiful."

"It's a little too late for that now, isn't it," she said with a smirk

"You and that mouth ma," he said with a smirk of his own.

"But, to answer your question, no. I do not have a man. I do, however, have a friend that's been around for a few months now," she said as she looked him directly in the eyes.

"I appreciate your honesty baby but, unfortunately, he will no longer be ya friend when we return from Miami," Block said with certainty as he stepped of the elevator into his home.

"How can you be so sure? I've known him longer than I have you. You're not gonna hurt him or nothing, are you?" she asked as she released his hand.

"Certainly not beautiful, it will be you that hurts him, his feelings that is. After one weekend with me, I guarantee you won't even look at another man," Block said with a cocky smile.

"Are you always this sure of yourself?" she asked.

"If I don't believe in myself, who will," he said, shrugging his shoulders. "This is our stop beautiful; if you could be so kind to remove your shoes please," he said, stepping to the side to let her get off first.

Chasity placed her suitcase by the wall in the hallway, so she could balance herself to remove her shoes. She looked around in awe at the scene before her; the Italian floors and the tall ceiling were gorgeous. Block picked up her roll-on suitcase, so his floors wouldn't get scuffed up from her pulling it around the house.

"Welcome to ma place, can I get you anything to drink sweetheart?" he asked, as he walked in the direction of the kitchen.

"No, I'm fine, thank you. Who did your decorating; it's breathtaking?" she asked, looking around the kitchen and dining room.

"Me, I got a little taste hun," he said as he placed her bags down to get a bottle of water and lemon out of the refrigerator.

"You did not," she said in disbelief.

"I sure did ma; let me give you a tour," Block said as he took her hand.

He took all of five minutes showing her around his 3-bedroom penthouse. In each room they passed, she was left speechless with her mouth hung open. She still couldn't believe that he designed the entire penthouse. Once they were done with the tour, she went through her bags and removed everything but her toiletries, sleepwear for the night, and an outfit to wake up with. That took her down to one carry-on bag. Block had since excused himself to go get dressed and to retrieve his own luggage. When he emerged from the master bedroom, he came out with two Louis Vuitton carry-on bags, one for each of them. Block was never the flashy type, but he did shine when it came to a few things; luggage just so happened to be one of them.

"Hey ma, you about ready to go?" he asked when he looked at the time. "Here, put your stuff in this sweetheart."

"No, I can't do that," she said, pushing the bag back towards him.

"Seriously ma, what I look like carry this and you carrying that? We gotta match each other's fly ma; if it will make you feel better, I will get you your own set when we get to Miami. So you won't feel bad about taking mine," he said with a wink. "Come on ma, we need to get a move on it or we gon be late for our flight," he said as he helped her up off the floor.

He did a once over to make sure he had everything; he checked again to make sure his gun was secure on his waist before making their way to the elevator. They both put on their shoes while waiting for the elevator to arrive. Once it did, they got on and made small talk the whole way down. She talked about all the places she visited on her last trip to Miami and also the places she didn't get a chance to see. Block made a mental note to take her to those places, once he got their initial plans out of the way. The drive over to the airport's private section was a smooth one filled with small talk and laughter, as they cruised at a fair speed through the Buffalo streets. She asked him questions about his love for black and white and his attraction to the fast life. He filled her in on his need to be able to provide abundantly for the ones he loved and his vision of the world being black and white, and that being the reason why he loved those colors. Block always said the world was either black or world with no grey areas in between. When it came to people, either you were on or off, good or bad. There was no such thing as a middle ground to him. Block wasn't a person that believed in fairy tales; he found out at an early age that life was what you made it. He witnessed his mother struggle; he saw her work two to three days in and day out, only to still struggle to make ends meet. He decided early on that he would do everything within his power to keep her from every struggling again in life and, so far, he had lived up to that promise.

When they arrived at the private side of the airport, Amir was standing by the plane, awaiting their arrival. He looked relieved to see them; he was sure they would be late, but they made it with five minutes to spare. Once they got out and he removed their bags from the car, he met up with Block and they came in for a brotherly embrace.

"My mannnn, I ain't seen you since last month's meeting; I thought you forgot about a nigga," Amir said, once he released Block.

"Damn, it been that long; shiddd, we gotta do better fam, but what's good my nigga? How you been?" asked Block.

"I'm making it. I'm making it, but who is this lovely young lady?" Amir asked, as he reached out to her for a handshake.

"This is my future wife, Chasity; she just doesn't see it yet," Block said with a smile.

"Well, she certainly knows it now; how are you Ms. Chasity? My name is Amir; me and this joker went to college together," he said, patting Block on the shoulder.

"Oh wow, I didn't know you went to college Chauncey," Chasity said, truly surprised.

"It's a lot of things you don't know about me, ma, but you will find out all you need to know in due time. Let's go ahead and board this plan before it takes off without us," Block said while placing his hand at the small of her back to guide her towards the plane's steps. He handed Amir a copy of his car key and told him to text him with the section and space number as to where he left it. They slapped hands one more time and he thanked him for coming through at the last minute for him. They boarded the plane and handed their bags to the private flight attendant that was at the top of the steps.

Once they got settled in their seats, the captain came out to speak to them and advised them of the plane's rules. They opted to turn their phones off, instead of putting them on airplane mode. The captain instructed them to put their seatbelts on and stay seated until he turned the seatbelt sign off. He also said it was okay to smoke, just as long as they waited until they were at the 30 thousand feet mark. Chasity decided to take a little power nap during their 2 ½ hour ride. He assured her that it was okay to rest, and he would wake her up once they arrived at their destination. He asked the attendant to get her a pillow, blanket, and an eye cover. With them flying private and not commercial, the seats could recline all the way back; there also was a bed available in the back, but she decided to stay up front with him.

When they reached the ideal height in the sky, Block lit up a blunt of Africa and smoked to calm his nerves. No matter how many times he did it, he would never be use to flying. Block always said if God wanted us to fly, then he would've given us wings. After smoking his blunt to the halfway point, he put the blunt out in the ashtray and decided to take a nap as well.

The flight attendant woke them both just minutes before the plane was to land. Block stood up to stretch his body; he asked the flight attendant for some mints or piece of gum; he thought it was rude to be in people's faces with a hot mouth. He looked over at Chasity as she rubbed the sleep from her eyes; even in her sleepy state with her hair out of place, she was still beautiful to him. He just loved to look at her; her beauty was unmatchable in his eyes. When the attendant returned with the mints, he put one in his mouth and gave the other one to Chasity. She laughed at his straight forward behavior, then went into the bathroom to freshen up a bit before they got off the plane. When she returned, Block was waiting by the stairs with their bags in hand. He asked if she was ready and she said yes; Chasity wasn't too fond of flying either.

There was a car waiting and ready to take them to their hotel on beachfront property when they ascended the stairs. The driver's name was Derrick, who stated that he would be at their disposal for the duration of their stay. Amir had covered all bases from the plane to the escort around town; Block was pleased with his ability to make things happen on such short notice. He made a mental note to pay his old friend a little something extra for his quick and thorough efforts. On the ride over to the hotel, Block asked if she wanted to stop and get anything to eat. She stated she was fine and rather order in; she was too tired to be cruising Miami's streets at close to 1 in the morning.

Once they arrived at the hotel, Block tipped Derrick and told him to be ready at 10am sharp. Derrick assured him he would and thanked him for his generosity. After checking in, Block asked the desk clerk if he could send up a platter of different appetizers, since he wasn't sure of what foods she liked. Of course, buffalo wings were one of the first items he ordered, since he knew she ate that much. Being the gentlemen that he was, Block allowed her to select the room of her choice first; both rooms were facing the beach, but she chose the one closest to the main exit. Block excused himself to his room to get settled and check his phone for missed message, but there were none. He wasn't sure if that was a good or bad thing, so he shot Leno a text just in case. He informed him that they made it safely and asked how everything was. Leno replied by saying all was well and for him to enjoy his vacation, and he would call if he needed him for any reason.

After a quick shower and comfortable clothes, Block made his way into the main room. He looked around and saw that the food had arrived, but Chasity was already working on her plate.

"Damn ma, it's like that?" Block said with a smile.

"Hun? Oh, you didn't miss much; it just got here. Plus, I was starving," Chasity said as she took a bite from a celery stick dipped in blue cheese.

"You could've let a nigga know something; hell, I'm hungry too," he said, taking a seat at the table.

"My bad son," Chasity said, laughing hard at her own joke.

"Yeah, you laughing cause you know that shit sounded wack as hell coming out ya mouth," he said with a laugh of his own. After a few minutes of silence, Block asked Chasity what she wanted to do tomorrow.

"Well, after we eat breakfast, I really need to go get some clothes, since you insisted that I leave behind the ones I originally had picked out," she said.

"Say no more sweetheart, I got you," he said as he continued to eat. They ate in silence for the remainder of their meal. They both were pretty tired after eating and decided it was best if they retired to the respected rooms for the night. Although, technically speaking, it was the next day since it was after midnight, but you know how black folks are; it's not tomorrow until you wake up and the sun is shining.

Block's alarm clock went off at 9am sharp. He got out the bed and stretched for a minute or two, then dropped right where he stood and did 2 sets of 50 push-ups. After a minor workout to get the blood flowing, he then went to the bathroom to handle his hygiene. He decided to wear a pair of denim shorts, a white t-shirt, and a pair of all white number 4 Jordan's. Block smelled of Creed cologne and fresh clean linen. Block was able to fit all of his clothes and shoes for the trip in one carry-on, unlike Chasity. His intentions were to spoil her this weekend and buy her everything her heart desired. He wanted to show her one of the many ways a queen was supposed to be treated and not just any queen, HIS queen.

He walked into the main room to make sure she was awake and ready for a fun filled day of sight-seeing and shopping, but what he saw before him made him stop in his tracks. There stood Chasity, next to a table filled with an assortment of fresh fruit and a breakfast fit for a king. Here he was planning to spoil her, but she had beat him to the punch. For Block, it was the simple things that meant the most to him; the things that a person didn't have to do but was thoughtful enough to do.

"Good morning beautiful, what's all this?" he asked with a smile, while pointing to the table as he walked in her direction. He grabbed her by the hips and pulled her close; he wrapped his arms around her lower back, then gently kissed her forehead.

"I just thought you might want to eat a hearty breakfast before we started with today's festivities," she said with a warm, yet breathless smile.

"Thank you, ma, that was sweet of you. I was gonna take you out for breakfast, but this is much better," Block said as he pulled out a chair for her; once she was seated, he took a seat directly across from her.

"I was hoping that we could hit the jet skis later sometime today," Chasity said with hope-filled eyes.

Block looked at her like she was crazy; he had no intentions of getting in what he liked to call live water. It was one thing to get in a swimming pool, a more controlled environment. But to be in live water, such as an ocean, was not something he wanted to do. But, the longer he looked at her face, the more excited she seemed to get. She even went as far as saying please over and over like a child would do their mother when begging for a toy at a toy store. He would never take that excitement and glee away from his queen, so he gave in to her demands. This was a quick vacation getaway; what is the point if you don't live a little and try new things?

"Sure sweetheart, we can do that," he said, regretting the words as soon as they left his mouth.

Chasity jumped around in her seat with excitement. She talked about how much she always wanted to do that; she even mentioned snorkeling, but Block wasn't having that. He refused to be that deep under water, just to look at fish; he suggested they visit an aquarium for that. She laughed at his statement and agreed that she wouldn't push him that far. They talked a little while longer as they ate a breakfast of pancakes, eggs, bacon, grits, fruit, and orange juice. Block opted not to eat the meat; he was sure the bacon wasn't turkey and he didn't eat pork. Block didn't partake in swine; he learned through his healthy eating and fitness coach years' prior that the pig was the nastiest animal to eat, so he hadn't eaten pork in over 5 years.

Chasity began to clear their plates and clean up the table as soon as breakfast was complete. Block offered to help, but she assured him she was fine and could handle it; she told him he could get the next set of dishes instead. He told her he was cool with that and used that time to call Leno to check in on their business. Leno told him everything was still all good, other than Detective Jackowski sitting outside of the spot on Ivy watching their every move. Block told him to shut it down and that he would be home in a few hours. Leno told him that he already handled it and to enjoy his time away. Leno asked him what sense did it make for him to come home when the issue had been addressed. He assured him that he could handle everything without him and that they had enough soldiers on standby, just in case shit got crazy. Block advised him to call if anything else popped off; if so, he was cutting the trip short and hauling ass back to Buffalo. They discussed a few more things, said their farewells, and ended the call. Block looked up from his phone to see Chasity sitting on the couch with her face in her phone, purse on her shoulder like she was ready to go.

"You ready to go beautiful?"

"I'm ready when you are baby," she said, standing to her feet.

"Okay, let me grab my stuff really quick," Block said as he jogged to his room to get his gun and wallet. He looked in his carry-on bag and grabbed a 10 thousand stack, then put the rest of the stacks of money in the safe. Making sure the safe was locked and secure, he then put the key in his wallet and went back to the main living space.

"Okay, I'm ready sweetheart," Block said to Chasity as they both made their way to the front door.

When they exited the main entrance, Derrick was ready and leaning against the car. It was almost 11am; Block wondered how long had he been standing outside in this heat. As they got closer, he noticed a bulge on Derrick's waist; he was strapped, just in case some funny shit went down. But, he wondered what a luxury car driver would need with a gun.

"Morning sir."

"Morning Derrick, how long have you been out here?" asked Block

"Since 9:45 this morning sir, didn't wanna be late," Derrick said as he opened the back door for Chasity.

"Good morning, and thank you," said Chasity, as she got in the car.

"Hey beautiful, give me few minutes to talk to Derrick okay," Block said, bending down to make eye contact.

"No problem boo," she said with a smile right before she closed the door.

"So, what kind of driving services does your company offer? And, by that, I'm referring to the piece you holding." Block said, taking a step closer to him.

"We offer special driving service to an elite group of people. My job is to drive you and your party wherever you please, as well as making sure you get there safely sir," Derrick said with a serious face and direct eye contact.

"I see," was all Block said.

"One Amir Rogers hired us sir; he said you would ask these questions as well," he said with a chuckle. "Just in case, he informed me to tell you and, I quote, 'GYC never travels alone no matter what state, country, or continent sir'," Derrick said with a smirk. He knew those words would put his mind at ease and make his job a lot easier.

"Ma nigga," Block said with a laugh in reference to Amir. "Ma bad son, you can't be too trusting these days, you feel me. But yo, if Amir sent you, then I know you one hundred," Block said, extending his hand for a fist bump.

"I understand, but I've known Amir for years; he's the reason I have this company. And when he called and said he needed my services for his friend, I told him I would handle it personally. Any friend of Amir is a friend of mine," Derrick said as he looked Block square in the eye.

"Real shit fam, I appreciate that too. But yo, we need to do some shopping; take us to the strip with all the high-end fashion stores."

"That would be Design District on 2nd Avenue over there between Midtown and Wynwood; that's a good 20 to 30-minute drive, but it's worth it," said Derrick.

"That's a bet," Block said, opening the door to get in the back seat.

Derrick nodded his head in acknowledgment, then walked around to the driver's side with haste to get them to their destination.

"You good sweetheart?" Block asked.

"Yes, I'm fine, thank you," she replied, never looking up from her phone.

"Alright, cool," Block said, putting on his shades and getting comfortable in his seat.

They arrived at their destination after a 30 to 40-minute ride. He thought they should start with a clothing store first, so he took her to Neiman Marcus for some retail therapy. She was apprehensive at first about the price of the items he picked out, but with him not taking no for an answer, she warmed up to the expensive gifts and soon followed suit. Block picked out a navy blue form fitting pantsuit by Donna Karen with a pair of peep toe red bottoms. A few pair of Seven and Robin's jeans later, they were headed to the Gucci store. He copped Chasity a bathing suit, a luggage set, 2 different colors of the latest released purses, a pair of big framed sunglasses to block the sun, and the haters, a set of Gucci guilty perfume and a set of Gucci by Gucci perfume with a keychain trinket and, lastly, he bought her a pair of heels and a belt. He also bought his sister Charmaine and his mother 2 purses a piece, since he was in Charmaine's favorite store. Before they headed out, he bought himself an all-black sweat suit and a pair of loafers, just in case he needed to dress grown man style while he was down here. After leaving the Gucci store, Chasity assured him that she had enough items and that she didn't need anything else, but he insisted on buying her at least one item out of every store on the strip. Chasity was thankful that she brought her comfortable sandals with her, or else she would have never been able to survive walking in stilettoes for that amount of time.

After shopping for two hours, Block thought they should take a break and stop for a light lunch. They decided to order a small salad and a bottled water from one of the restaurants in the outside food court. They made small talk in between bites about this and that, before hitting a few more stores and calling it quits for the day. Chasity suggested that they have a few drinks once they got back to the hotel before they hit the jet skis. Block told her he wasn't much of a drinker, but he was down to smoke a blunt or two before then. Once they got back to the hotel, Block told her to hold on a second while he got a cart to carry all their bags on. When they got up to the room, he placed all her bags in her bedroom, then he went in his to roll up a blunt to smoke on the patio right outside of his bedroom. He removed his shirt and pants to get a little more comfortable before his private smoke session began. He then looked at his phone to see if he had any missed notifications; only seeing one from his sister, Charmaine, he texted her back that he was out of town on business, and he would call her once he returned home.

There was a soft knock on the door that broke Block away from his concentration of blunt rolling; he looked back in the direction of the door and told her to come in.

"Hey you, what are you back here doing so secretly?" Chasity asked as she opened the door.

"Just rolling up, I was about to step out on the back patio beach area; care to join me beautiful lady?" Block asked with a smile as he applied his finishing touches to his Dutch master.

"I've never been big on smoking, but I'll give it a try since we're in the sunshine state," she said.

"Naw, you good ma, no need in hurting your virgin lungs with this shit," Block said, getting up and walking towards the patio door.

"I said I was never fond of smoking; I never said I didn't try it before. So pass the spiff, my nigga," Chasity said with a smile.

"Yea, you definitely not a smoker using words like spiff and shit," Block said with a laugh.

"Man, spark up and pass the dutchie to the left hand side my friend," Chasity said while breaking out into laughter.

"Man, you definitely not getting none of this good shit now," said Block with a laugh.

"Whatever," Chasity said, pulling a mini bottle of Hennessy out of her pocket. "It's six o' clock somewhere," she laughed as she twisted the cap and turned the bottle up til it was all gone. "AHHHH, now that will put some hair on your chest," she said as she fanned her mouth.

"You better than me shit; I can't drink no shit like that," Block said with passing her the blunt.

Chasity took a hit and instantly began coughing; Block patted her back while laughing and asking was she okay. She shook her head yes and continued on with their get-high session. A blunt and a half later, they were suited and booted ready to hit the jet skis.

Chasity looked over at a nervous Block and asked was he okay, while laughing. He replied yes with a nervous grin as they both listened to the instructor give them the do's and don'ts of riding a jet ski. As they entered the water, Block became more nervous as he started to have a change of heart. Chasity noticed his apprehension and decided it was best if they rode together the first go round. Block wouldn't dare protest to her suggestion, since she was driving and he was able to sit behind her with his hands wrapped around her waist while being close to her backside. Being the man that he was, after a few ripples of waves in the water had her ass bouncing up and down on his lap, it caused his dick to become slightly hard. The temptation was hard for him; Block tried to be a gentleman, but it was difficult for him to do so with a beautiful woman and her nice round ass bouncing up and down in his lap. Chasity looked back at him after feeling the hardness of his manhood, with a wink and a smile. She wouldn't protest either, with her attraction to him growing stronger by the minute. Chasity knew what she was doing to him but, truth be told, she kind of liked it.

Block wanted to drive the jet ski by himself the second go round; he had built up enough confidence watching Chasity and the way she handled her jet like a pro. If he didn't know any better, he would have thought this wasn't her first time riding. When they returned to shore to get the other jet ski for Block, he complimented her on her ability to ride.

"Thanks for not killing me back there; you sure this is your first time riding a jet ski?" Block asked as he got on.

"I'm positive, I just so happen to be good at riding things," Chasity said with a devilish smile as she took off.

With a smile of his own, Block pulled off, headed in her direction. Her excitement for fun was starting to rub off on him, making him smile and unwind more. This was what he needed, him being able to let his guard down a little more and enjoy the fruits of his labor. Even if not but for a moment, Block would enjoy his weekend to the fullest because once he returned back to Buffalo, it was business as usual, back to being the watchful, non-trusting, hustler that he had grown to be. Block had a plan to make her fall for him in just one short weekend and, so far, he was confident that his plan was working.

After 2 hours of jet skiing, they both decided that they had enough of playing in the water for now. The light snack that they ate earlier was starting to wear off and they both was ready for a meal that would stick to their bones. Their high had officially come down and Block was slowly getting sleepy. He wouldn't dare mention it though. He wanted her to have as much fun as she could; he would have stayed in the water for ten hours if that was what Chasity wanted. Nevertheless, he was thankful when she mentioned being hungry.

"So, what do you have a taste for?" Block asked as they walked back up their private beach to go inside to get cleaned up.

"No pressure, dealer's choice," Chasity said, removing the villa key from her bra.

"Wish I was them keys," Block said out loud, thinking he said it to himself.

"I bet you do," Chasity said with a laugh as she walked in the direction of her room. "Give me a good twenty minutes and I'll be ready to go," she said as she closed the door behind herself.

Block made his way to his room as well; he decided to smoke a blunt before he got in the shower. Thankfully, there was still half a blunt left in the ashtray, so he didn't have to roll up one. He sat and reflected on today's events while he smoked; he had to admit that he really enjoyed himself today. After he got over his initial fear of live water, he experienced a euphoric high like never before. The thrill of speeding, mixed with the sounds of nature and the motion from the ocean waves, really put Block in a calm state; a feeling he hadn't felt in quite a while. It seemed like for the last few months or so, him and Leno had been experiencing some hardship in one way or another. From the police robbing them to them having to kill a few niggas here and there but, either way, it was always something going on. That's why this trip was desperately needed. He needed some time away from it all, just to get a true peace of mind. He was hoping he could fully enjoy his vacation without having to cut it short on the count of some bullshit. He knew Leno could handle whatever came his way, but he also knew that Leno would shoot first and ask questions later, which most of the time wasn't the best way to go, but it's the only way he knew.

Finishing up the rest of the blunt, Block went to take a quick shower, so they could go eat. He thought today would be a good day to break out the cream colored linen short set his mom got him for Christmas last year, an outfit he wouldn't be caught dead in, in Buffalo. But, it was perfect to wear with this Miami weather and grown man enough to wear to the five-star restaurant he wanted to take Chasity to this evening. He paired it with his Gucci loafers and Gucci shades, along with his Gucci Guilty cologne. As he looked in the mirror to give himself the once over, Block came to the conclusion that he actual liked what he saw. He was feeling the grown man swag; it would definitely compliment the new direction he was trying to move in. He was slowly growing tired of the fast life. He was tired of looking over his shoulder, not knowing if today would be the last day he'd be alive, or his last day as a free man. He was ready to get married and start a family. All Block wanted was his peace of mind, his happy ending, his good old American dream.

Block emerged from his room looking and feeling like brand new money. He looked around the living room for Chasity but didn't see her. He was just about to go knock on her bedroom door when she walked into the main room, looking like she was ready to rip the runway. She wore an olive green bandage dress with a pair of nude and red Jimmy Choo pumps. A nude and red clutch purse with gold and red accessories to finish off her look. Block stood there in awe at the sight before him; to say she was sexy was an understatement. She was downright gorgeous. Her hair was up in a high bun, with a Chinese bang that stopped right above her eyebrows. Block had a thing for a woman with a long neck; it was one of his favorite spots to kiss on a woman. She politely smiled at him and cleared her throat, to let him know he was staring to long.

"You look amazing ma," Block said with lustful eyes.

"You clean up pretty well yourself," Chasity said as she blushed with a smile.

"You ready to go sweetheart?"

"I sure am, lead the way future," Chasity said with her arms extended towards the door.

Block looked back at Chasity with a sexy smirk; she really was starting to grow on him. He loved everything about her, from her beautiful eyes to her sexy sassy mouth. Boy, oh boy, the things he wanted to do to that mouth of hers. Block shook his head to free himself from his nasty thoughts, so he could focus more on his date for the evening. He had a few tricks up his sleeve tonight and he didn't want any distractions. So, he would just have to push his wants and desires to the back of his mind for now.

Derrick was ready and waiting for them out front, with strict instructions to drive around the block a few times to give the staff time to get everything ready for the evening. Before getting into the car, Block asked Chasity to put on the blindfold that he gave her just as they were walking up to the car. She was skeptical at first but obliged him, since he went through the trouble of surprising her. Block was anxious; he couldn't wait to see the look on her face when she realized that the five-star restaurant was really their hotel villa made up to look like one. He had everyone on standby, waiting for their que.

Once front desk saw them leave, they went straight to work, getting the inside and their personal beach setup. He got the idea earlier when they came back from jet skiing. He shot Amir a text, telling him what he wanted to do, and Amir made it happen. Block had intentions on making this a night that she would always remember. Their night consisted of a meal cooked by an exclusive celebrity chef, full body massages on the beach, followed by a night of dancing at an exclusive night club and lounge. A celebrity guest list with a reservation and invitation only, something Amir was able to pull off at the last minute due to him investing in the owner's business idea. Amir was proving to be more of an asset as the day went on; he was a man of action and that's something Block could appreciate. Amir never ceased to amaze him with his connections and his can do attitude. Block really valued their friendship, as well as his opinion and his business savvy mind.

After riding around for fifteen minutes or so, Block finally got the call that he been waiting on. Felicia from front desk called to say everything was set and ready to go, and that they were just awaiting their arrival. Block thanked her and disconnected the call. He looked up and gave Derrick a head nod, signaling to him that everything was a go. Derrick nodded his head in agreement and made his way back towards the hotel. Block looked over at Chasity sitting in silence, her chest heaving up and down, her legs shaking with anticipation. He reached over to her and gently touched her leg; he whispered in her ear, telling her that there was no reason to be nervous. He kissed her on the cheek ever so softly while continuing to rub her leg to relax her.

When they pulled up to the front of the hotel, Block put his hand up to stop Derrick from getting out the car. He wanted to be the one to guide her out the car and up the steps to the surprise that awaited her. Block grabbed her hand and slid slowly to the side, making his way to the door from the backseat. After he got out, he reached for her hand to pull her out as well. Placing one hand in hers and the other in the small of her back, he helped her onto the sidewalk and up the stairs. Walking pass the front desk, he smiled and winked at Felicia as a gesture to say thank you; she smiled back and nodded her head in acknowledgement. Block opened their villa door and stepped aside after removing her blindfold. Chasity looked on in awe at the sight before her. Rose petals adored every inch of the entryway, along with tea light candles. She stood still for a few moments with a shocked expression; her mouth slightly open, forming an O. She turned around with misty eyes and came face to face with Block, who was waiting her reaction. She hadn't even seen the whole setup and she was already appreciative of what she'd seen thus far. She reached in for a hug and kissed him gently on the lips before pulling away. She looked him in the eyes before thanking him and telling him how sweet he was and how no one had ever done anything like that for her before.

As they walked further into the main room, they came across a candlelit table for two, with a makeshift menu next to their plates. Block pulled out her chair for her, then placed a cloth napkin over her lap. A waiter came up to the table just as Block took his seat. He had a bottle of finely aged wine in hand; he poured each of them a glass, told them his name was Josh, and asked if they wanted to start off with a soup, salad, or oysters for an appetizer. Block opted for a salad and Chasity went with the oysters; Josh told him he would be back momentarily, then disappeared to the kitchen. Chasity went on to tell him how much she loved seafood and a number of other foods that she was fond of. Before long, Josh returned with their appetizers and the chef in tow. He introduced himself as Mikel; he studied under a five-star chef in Paris for seven years. He stated that he had an exclusive restaurant in south beach Miami that required a reservation with a six month waiting list. He was here doing a favor for his friend, Amir, who helped him get his business off the ground. He went over the menu with them, which consisted of three choices;

veal steak with blue king crab legs, grilled tilapia with a sweet basil tomato sauce and asparagus, and grilled chicken with an Alaskan sweet onion sauce seared with Alaskan snow crab, followed by homemade raspberry lemon iced tea to drink. All the items were ready and prepared just one hour prior to his arrival. Chasity was having a hard time choosing, so Block opted for a sample of all three for them. This made Mikel smile; he was hoping they would say this as he had already prepared for this answer. He kept the items in a preheated carrier, allowing the food to stay piping hot until it arrived at its destination. Mikel excused himself to go prepare their food for presentation; he was big on that. He was taught that it was all in the way you presented the food to the guests; people tended to flock to a five-star restaurant for the appearance and experience, more so then the actual food they ordered. It was all about status for most people, but Mikel took pride in his work. Cooking was a form of art to him and, with each plate he prepared, he strived to create a masterpiece.

While Mikel was busying himself in the kitchen, Block took this time to get to know her better; he asked her what were her dreams, goals, and aspirations. Then he asked what he could do to help achieve the things she wished to do. Chasity's heart skipped a beat when he asked her that; never had she been asked that question before by any man or woman, for that matter. She stared intensely in his eyes as he sat back and awaited her answer; she smiled and told him to remain loyal and that she had the rest covered. He was okay with that answer for now, but there was no way Block would sit back and not help his queen accomplish her dreams. It just wasn't the type of man he was; he preferred to be hands on with his woman, no matter how unimportant it seemed to everyone else.

Mikel and Josh entered the room with a meal fit for royalty in hand. Block got excited at the sight before him, so much so that he was unknowingly rubbing his hands together with anticipation. Mikel placed their respective plates in front of them and took two steps back to allow them space to dig in. Whenever he did a special dinner, he always stood by the table as his guests took the first bite; it brought him great joy to see their facial expression as they did so.

Chasity decided to dig into the seafood portion first; she slightly moaned after a small bite of the blue king crab. She gave Mikel a look of shear bliss and happiness; she just loved to eat, especially if the food was prepared well. Block smiled to himself as he cut into his veal. It was like cutting butter; with very little effort, he was able to slice off a small portion to taste. He shook his head up and down as he began to chew; he looked Mikel in the eyes and gave him a thumbs up. He never ate veal before, but he could understand why it was such an expensive meat. Mikel was satisfied with their gestures, so he removed himself to allow them privacy. Josh sat down two glasses of iced tea with fresh raspberry and lemon in them. He asked Chasity if she needed a refill of her wine and she shook her head yes; Block, on the other hand, had not touched his. Chasity pleaded with him to take a sip of his wine, stating that it was the best wine she had ever tasted. He refused at first but, remembering that they were on vacation, he decided to take a sip or two to oblige her request. It was indeed very good, but Block just wasn't big on drinking like that. Maybe if they were in for the night, he would have had a little more, but he refused to be in public if he had been drinking; he didn't want to be caught off guard. You would think them being out of state would make a difference, but old habits were hard to break, so he opted not to.

After dinner, Mikel made a homemade strawberry shortcake and caramel cake for desert. They were only able to take a few more bites before they were calling it quits from being full. Mikel made sure to wrap up what was leftover, along with a fresh fruit bowl and homemade whipped cream, just in case there would be a need for a late night snack. After cleaning up the kitchen while they sat at the table talking, he excused himself for the night, along with Josh thanking them for allowing him to cook for them. Block stood up to walk them to door and handed them each a two-hundred-dollar tip, thanking them for being available in such short notice and the well cooked meal. He locked the door behind them, then went back to the table to resume his talk with Chastity. She talked about how much she was enjoying herself so far and how good the meal was.

Block looked Chasity in the eyes with a more serious facial expression and asked her did she trust him. She looked him directly in the eye and said that she did with her life. That was all he needed to hear; he scooted back in his chair and helped her out of hers. He walked her to her bedroom door and told her to get completely naked and to use the bathrobe on her bed to cover up once she was done. She looked concerned at first but, the more she looked into his eyes, the more her heart and concern melted away. Block told her to be ready in five minutes; he was going to do the same.

They emerged from their rooms at the same time, and Block asked Chasity to, once again, close her eyes as he guided her to the back patio towards the beach. When she opened them, she was standing in front of a makeshift cabana with massage chairs and Sade softly playing in background. She smiled to herself as she walked up to shake hands with the massage therapist, Kelly, who would be working on her tonight. They both were instructed to remove their robe and to lie in the chair face down. She couldn't help but to look him up and down when he took off his robe; his chiseled chest and arms was causing a lump to form in her throat. She found herself clutching her chest, as if she was having a heart attack; something about this man just took her to a dark and nasty place. She had recently started fantasizing about being with him sexually and all the things she wanted him to do to her body. And seeing him stark naked didn't make it any better.

Block noticed her staring; he thought it was cute how she tried her best to hide the attraction she had to him; he, on the other hand, could not.

"See something you like ma?" Block asked with a sexy smirk.

"No comment," Chasity said with a laugh. "Let me enjoy this much needed massage; it's been a while since I've had my body rubbed."

"I think I can accommodate you on that on a regular basis."

"I be you can," Chasity said with a smirk while settling in for her massage.

"Sorry to interrupt, but let's get started," said Kelly. "To get the maximum experience, it's best that you remain silent and put your mind, body, and soul in a calm state. Find your happy play and go there; honestly speaking, you shouldn't have to do much since we are on this beautiful beach," Kelly said with a pause. "Would you all like some fruit or champagne before we get started?"

"I would love another glass of the wine we had at dinner," said Chasity.

"Not a problem, let me go get that for you; in the meantime, you just lie here and relax. Would you like for me to cover you while I'm gone momentarily?" Kelly asked, grabbing a sheet.

"No, I'm fine, thank you; that ocean breeze feels wonderful against my skin," Chasity said as she turned her head to face Block's direction.

"Very well, be back in a jiffy," said Kelly as she motioned for her partner, Brooke, to come with her to give them some privacy.

"You're not going to make this easy on me, are you?" Block asked, adjusting his member as he rolled over on his back.

Chasity looked over at the sight before her and took in a deep breath. She knew he was working with something from the ride on the jet skis, but to see it just standing at attention and him be unbothered was doing something to her. It was like he knew exactly what he was doing, and that he wanted her to look at him. Her suspicions were confirmed when he grabbed his member and began to stroke it lightly, all while looking her directly in the eye. Chasity couldn't believe her eyes; never had she seen a man jack off in front of her before. Block stroked himself for another thirty seconds or so, while he laid there making love faces and teasing her. He decided to end his game of sexual torture when he saw Kelly and her associate walking up in the distance. He would just have to finish his act another time or, perhaps, take his show on the road later tonight. He turned to lie back on his stomach and tucked his dick between it and the lounge chair. He looked over at Chasity with a wicked smirk and winked at her before turning his head to face the other direction, as if nothing ever happened.

Chasity was honestly happy for the distraction; a few more seconds and she would have jumped on him and finished the job herself. She didn't want to appear thirsty or desperate, but it had been a long time since she'd felt a man's touch, and she was long overdue. Had Block met her eight or so years ago, he would have most likely gotten the goods on the first night, but she had since then changed for the better. Chasity now understood the value of self-worth and loving yourself enough to respect yourself first and foremost.

"Here you go hun," Kelly said to Chasity.

"Thanks," Chasity said, finishing the glass off in what seemed like one gulp.

193

"Okay, well I thought we should start with a quick rub down, just to kind of relax the muscles a bit. Then move on to the hot rock massage, followed by the acupuncture technic," Kelly as she explained her itinerary for their two-hour massage session.

After their session was over, Chasity stated that she wanted to go and take a quick shower before they continued on with the night's festivities. Block agreed and returned to his room as well to do the same; plus, he needed to take a cold shower and release the nut he had been holding back. He heard a knock at the door while he was in the shower; he yelled out that he was coming and to give him a few more minutes. He was in the process of pleasuring himself when she knocked, but he turned the water off, grabbed a towel, and wrapped it around his lower half before opening the door.

"What's wrong ma?" he asked, noticing that she wore a house coat.

"That massage got me feeling too relaxed, and I'm not sure what else you have planned for the night, but I thought that maybe we could just stay in and get to know each other better," said Chasity with a seductive look in her eye.

Block was all too familiar with that look; he'd seen the look of lust too many times in the faces of other women that he'd came across. He was all for staying in and seeing where the night would lead; he just hoped that Amir hadn't gone through too much trouble to get them on the guest list for club Exclusive.

"That's cool baby girl; just give me a few minutes to throw something on and call Derrick to cancel and I'll be right out."

"You sure I can't watch?" Chasity asked while sucking on her finger seductively.

"You ain't said nothing but a word ma," Block said as he released his towel, letting it fall, freeing his hard member and allowing it to stand at attention. He would have to call Derrick later; maybe give him a good tip and he'd forget all about him canceling without calling.

Chasity looked him up and down while licking her lips as she untied her robe and let it drop to the floor as well. Wearing nothing but her bra and panties, she stopped and stood still, allowing him a moment to take in her beauty. Thinking to herself that it was now or never, she reached out and touched his face, then pulled him in for a kiss.

Kissing him with so much passion as if he was her soldier husband who'd just returned home from war, she damn near swallowed his lips whole. There was no question about it; she wanted him bad. I'm talking Wale bad, and he wanted her just as bad. Block wasn't big on kissing, but the thing she was doing with her tongue made his knees buckle. Unable to take it any longer, Block lifted her off her feet and wrapped her legs around his waist. With their lips still locked together, he carried her over to the bed and laid her down gently; he pulled her panties down to her ankles and removed them completely. He put them to his nose and took a big sniff, like he was trying to remember her scent, quite like a hound dog would do. Chasity lightly laughed; she found it strange that he was so free with his emotions, but she loved it at the same time. She had never met a man that wasn't afraid to express his feelings so free heartedly; he wasn't scared to go after what he wanted. His confidence in them was what made it easy for her to be free and follow his lead. She knew in her heart that he wouldn't purposely hurt her; she was more afraid of him being the one getting hurt. Her past was a checkered one, and her closet was full of skeletons that she wanted to keep hidden forever. But, with Block being the man like she heard he was, it was only a matter of time before he found out. She just hoped that he would love the woman she'd become and not hate the woman she used to be. Chasity broke free from her thoughts of the past when she felt a pair of lips on the tips of her toes.

"Do you trust me?" Block asked while looking down at Chasity with an intense glare.

"Yes, I can't explain why, but I just do," she said, wondering where he was going with his line of questioning. She thought he would be more focused on the soaking wet pussy that was lying before him; now was not the right time to be asking questions.

"Can you see yourself with me and only me?" he asked, still holding her foot up to his lips while talking in between her toes.

"Yes."

"So, from this day forward, it's me and you, right? Block asked, flicking his tongue repeatedly between the big toe and her second toe.

"Ahhhhh yes, I trust you baby, it's me and you baby, against the world baby, pleasssssse," Chasity cried out in between breaths.

"Please what? What you begging for ma; I ain't even did nothing to you yet ma. Just you wait," he said before he stuck her big toe all the way in his mouth while using his tongue to play with it.

"OH MY GODDDD!" Chasity screamed out, unaware of how good it felt to have her toes sucked. She should have known he was a certified freak when he jacked his dick in front of her.

"Mmm hmm," Block said before he removed her foot from his mouth. He spread her legs wide open to see her pink pussy soaking wet; her juices had already formed a small puddle under her butt. "I want you to know that, as soon as I put my mouth on this, you belong to me. This is now mines and no other man can touch it, taste it, smell it, or see it. Do you understand and agree?" Block asked, pointing to her and her pussy.

"I understand, baby pleassse, I'm so ready," she said while shaking her head up and down, unable to keep still. She was just about to cum and she wanted him to bring that feeling back.

"Ma, I need to you look at me when I say this because I'm only going to say this once. If you allow me to be your man, we will never use condoms and, trust me when I say that, I will never sleep with anyone else. You may want to get on birth control if you don't want any children right now because I will never pull out. If it is truly mine, I will plant all of my seeds inside of you; my seeds will never go to waste. If you suck my dick and I cum in your mouth, you will swallow it up; I eat healthy enough with minimum salt, so I'm sure that it tastes sweet. This weekend and this weekend only will be the only time that I will pull out; if you must, you can handle the birth control issue when we get home. Are you okay with these terms and conditions?" Block asked with a serious look in his face.

Chasity sat up on the bed to process everything that he just said. "Yes, I'm okay with them, but the whole raw dog thing, I'm not too sure about," she stated honestly.

"I thought you would say that, good answer though," he said as he walked over to his carry-on bag and pulled out some papers and handed them to her.

Chasity looked over the papers with wide eyes for a minute or two. She was amazed at his clean bill of health, getting his checkup every six months. He'd never had so much as a cold, let alone an STD. She was more amazed that he would carry it around with him. "Wow, okay, well since your most recent checkup was last month, have you slept with anyone unprotected since then?" she asked, already knowing the answer to her own question, one that Block felt he did not have to answer, so he just looked at her with the *really* face.

"My question for you is, are you clean as well?" he asked as he looked her in the eyes.

"Yes, I am; I had my annual six months ago and I haven't had sex with anyone in over a year. So, it's safe to say that I'm clean as well," she stated as she stood up with her hands on her hips.

"I believe you ma, and I trust you as well," he said in between kisses on her neck and collarbone. "I just had to get that out the way because I come behind no man in life, especially when it comes to pussy, you feel me? And just so you know ma, if I get any diseases, I will gladly kill you with no hesitation, as if you never mattered to me. Do you understand?"

"Yes, I understand," she said with a serious tone.

"Good, now lay back and let daddy see his pussy," Block said with a devilish smile.

"Owww, you so nasty, but I like that," she said with a sexy smile.

"Ohhh, you have no idea how nasty I can be ma, but your're bout to find out," Block said as he got down on his knees.

He opened her legs as wide as they could go, then spread her second set of lips open as well. He wanted to see how pink it was, while he also discreetly checked for bumps and scars. Happy with his findings, he went straight to her clit and attacked it like a wild hungry animal. He licked and sucked on her clit like it was his last meal, devouring every ounce of her sweet nectar to quench his thirst. Just as she was getting ready to explode, he reached up and grabbed her legs, wrapping them around his neck, and stood to his feet while continuing his assault in the air. Holding her up by her butt for extra support, Block continued to give her the tongue lashing of her life. Chasity raised her hands high above her head, using the ceiling to help balance and support herself. Never in her life had she felt pleasure such as this. She already had a powerful orgasm when he first lifted her up in the air; juices were flowing from her thighs and down his chest, making him work harder to bring her to ecstasy. Block felt her legs tighten up around his neck, which to him was a sign of her getting ready to climax yet again. He used his middle finger to collect some of her juices to get his finger good and wet. Just as he felt her pussy muscles contracting on his face, he slowly slid his middle finger in her ass to enhance her experience. He could feel her body tense up at first but, as quickly as she tensed up, her body began to quickly relax when he used his ring finger to finger her pussy at the same time. At that point, Chasity lost all use of her legs and upper body strength as she called on Jesus, Buda, Allah and every god known to mankind.

"Nah, don't go limp on me now; I ain't nowhere near through with that ass. Hold on tight ma," Block said.

He then lifted her off his neck and shoulders and turned her body counter clockwise, so they could pleasure each other at the same time.

"OH MY GOD, wait baby, I can't, I can't, I just cannnttt!" Chasity cried out as he spun her around.

"You can't what ma? What, you can't give ya man no head? What you can't do; let a nigga know ma," Block said as he licked from her ass to her pussy, knowing it was driving her crazy.

"I don't think I can come anymore; I can't take it," she said, panting and breathing heavy.

"You can take it baby; now come on and suck this dick before I drop yo ass on ya head," said Block with a laugh.

Chasity did as she was told; she had never given head upside down before. The blood was starting to rush to her head, but she continued to suck his dick like the pro she was. Little did Block know, he wasn't the only freak in the room. She'd had her fair share of sex partners, so she was far from new to the freak shit. But this time felt different; this time, it felt real. She could feel the love oozing from his tongue and she loved every minute of it. That's why it was only right that she returned the favor and show him just who he was fucking with. Chasity wrapped her arms around his waist and slowly slid all ten of his inches into her mouth. His dick was so deep down her throat that she began to hum and he felt the vibrations all the way down to his balls.

The feeling she was giving him made his knees buckle. She popped his dick out her mouth and looked back at him, asking him if he was okay. He nodded his head yes and motioned for her to continue doing what she was doing. Block made the fatal mistake of thinking she was an amateur; he just knew he would have to upgrade her sexually. Boy, was he wrong; Chasity's head game was superb, and her throw it back game was even better.

"Shit, if the pussy as good as the head, I'll marry that bitch tomorrow," Block thought to himself.

Chasity got back in the mode of pleasing him; to her, there was an art to dick sucking and she definitely mastered it. She enjoyed giving sloppy toppy; she made nasty slurping noises as she spit and sucked, twisted and pulled on his member, making him lose control.

"Shidd ma, it's like that? Aight, lay that ass down," Block said, referring to the head he just received as he put her down on her feet.

He gave her a minute or two to rest, so the blood could properly circulate throughout her body. He didn't want her to pass out from hanging upside down too long.

"You good ma?" he asked.

"Yeah, I'm just about there; I was getting light headed for a second. But I'm good now, thank you."

"Thank me later after I demolish that pussy; now, lay back and let daddy do his job," Block said with a wicked smile.

Block climbed on the bed and hovered over her body, resting between her legs. He leaned in for an intimate kiss; while she was wrapped up in the passion of their kiss, Block entered her realm slowly, yet forcefully. She was super wet but extra tight; he could tell it had been a while since a man had been in it.

"Sssss, damn ma, that thang super tight; it's hugging the shit out of my dick," Block said as his eyes rolled to the back of his head from sheer pleasure. "You bet not ever give this pussy away; this shit belongs to me now; do you understand?" Block asked through gritted teeth while he increased his speed and depth in her.

"Yes, oh my god yesssssss! I understand baby; I un-der-stand," she said in between heavy breaths.

"Turn over ma, I want you face down with that ass up."

Turning over and arching her back as high up as she could, Chasity jiggled her ass, showing him that she was ready.

"Oh shit, throw that ass back ma," Block said, slapping her on the ass while she twerked on his dick.

It was something about a woman who knew how to throw it back. Unable to hold out any longer, Block pulled out and spilled his seeds all over her ass, then collapsed beside her on the bed. They laid there silently for a minute or two, while catching their breath and staring into each other's eyes. She leaned in for a passionate kiss before going into the bathroom to relieve herself and shower. Block entered the bathroom minutes later to take a piss and join her in the shower. Grabbing the loofah, he poured a generous amount on it and proceeded to wash her back.

"That feels sooo good," she moaned.

"You like that?" Block whispered in her ear from behind as he moved on to a more sensitive area.

Unable to speak, Chasity shook her head yes as she leaned back into him. She couldn't believe that she was even considering going for a round two after the explosive lovemaking session they'd just had. But, truth be told, she couldn't get enough. He was the most attentive lover she'd ever had and, not to mention, the biggest. She'd must have slept with at least thirty guys, but none of them could compare to him and his exceptional lovemaking skills. Now she understood why some women called their man daddy in the bedroom. He had her feeling helpless like a baby.

"Mmm hmm, now say thank you, daddy," Block said with a sexy grin.

"Thank you for what?"

"For this good dick I'm about to feed you, ma," he said with a laugh.

"If it's good like you say it is, I'll thank you after," she said with a grin of her own.

"Say no more," Block said as he forcefully bent her over and slid into her dripping honeycomb hideout.

"OH MY DAMN!" she cried out in pleasure.

They made love until the water turned cold and their skin looked old. Block gave her that thug loving all night long, round after round until the sun came up. They made love in the kitchen, on the floor on top of the bearskin rug, and even on the beach.

They slept in late and ate leftovers for breakfast. They both were famished, due to the intense love making from the night before. After getting dressed and putting on some more relaxed clothing, Chasity wanted to use their last day in Miami for sightseeing and visiting historical places in the city. Block apologized to Derrick for not canceling and gave him a five-hundred-dollar tip for the inconvenience once they reached the car. He insisted it was fine and that he only waited two hours past the time he was scheduled to be there. Block just sat back and enjoyed the ride as she instructed Derrick to take her to all the places that she wanted to see. They were scheduled to leave at noon the next day, and Block planned on relaxing, fucking, and having a smoke out session on the beach for the remainder of the evening on their last night in Miami.

"Come on ma, our plane will be here in an hour; are you sure you got everything?" Block yelled out into the next room.

"I'm doing a double sweep now daddy; give me a few minutes!" she yelled back.

"You know a nigga love that daddy shit; keep it up and I'm a bend your ass over the couch."

"Don't you threaten me with a good time," Chasity said, peeking her head through the open bedroom door and smiling.

"Aight then, let's go ma; Miami was cool but a nigga starting to feel home sick. Plus, this nigga Leno ain't answer the phone none yesterday or this morning and I'm jive starting to get worried," Block said, now pacing the floor back and forth.

"Who's name did you say?" Chasity asked with a concerned look on her face.

"My right hand man Leno; why, you know him or something?" Block asked.

"Um naw, I though you said someone else; let me finish up, so we can go," Chasity said, quickly exiting the room.

"You have got to be fucking kidding me," Chasity said aloud to herself.

She used to mess around with a dude by that name a few years back. The name was too rare for it to be a different Leno; it had to be the same one. And if that was the case, she was sure that Block would find out about her sketchy past. She went by a different name back then; back then, everyone called her by her middle, which was Onyx. The only thing that could save her was for her to hold off on meeting his friends for at least six months or more. She though that would buy her enough time for Block to truly fall in love with her, making it easier for him to see beyond her past and forgive her for being somewhat deceitful. Until then, she would be everything that he needed and more. She was almost sure that she'd finally found the man that she could spend the rest of her life with, and she would hate to lose him over some mistakes that she made as a young adult. She had only known him for three short days but, from day one, he made her feel special. He had truly made her feel like a queen; no man had ever gone through such great lengths to make her feel wanted, valued, and loved the way that he had in such a short amount of time. Not even her ex-boyfriend, Geechee, who she was with for two years. Block interrupted her thoughts with a knock on the door.

"Hey ma, you good in here?"

"Yea, I'm almost done in here!" Chasity yelled out from the bathroom as she picked up the last of her toiletries

"Alright now beautiful, you got about five more minutes, then I'm leaving ya ass," he said with a chuckle as he walked back into the direction of the living area.

"And if you do, I swear, Chauncey, I will never talk to you again," she said with her lip poked out.

"Well then, hurry yo ass up."

"Whatever nigga," she laughed.

Arriving to the airport in the nick of time, Block helped Chasity out the car and told her to go ahead and board, that he would get their bags. He took a moment to properly thank Derrick by handing him an envelope with two-thousand-dollar cash tip inside. They slapped hands and exchanged phones numbers, with Derrick telling him to call him if he ever needed him for anything. He assured him that he knew at least one person in every line of business, and that he would always be available to help. Block thanked him again and assured him that he would do so. It was always good to make a new ally in this business, especially one that was old school who still believed in the silent code of the streets. He was certain that Amir would never connect him with an untrustworthy person. Even when Block was relaxing, he was never truly relaxing; he was still aware of his surroundings. He noticed Derrick doing the same as well; he noticed that he always stood in a position to watch all sides and exits, as well as watching for faces and body language. Derrick was always on point, a true street nigga turned business, something Block could appreciate since he had done the same.

Thirty minutes into the ride, Block grabbed Chasity by the hand and took her to the bed area that was located at the back of the plane. He asked her if she wanted to join the mile-high club and proceeded to lift up her dress and enter her from the back. Surprisingly, she was soaking wet, like she was waiting on him to take the pussy. Their love making session lasted all of fifteen minutes, then they went back to their seats and made idle conversation until the plane landed.

"Yo son, I appreciate everything you did to make this mini vacation successful," Block said as he dapped Amir up. "Check your account on Wednesday; I'm a have you straightened out good."

"Aww man, ain't no thang, this what I do," said Amir as he returned the gesture. "How you doing miss lady?"

"I'm fine, so I have you to thank for the lovely time I had in Miami?" asked Chasity with a genuine smile.

"All I did was book the flight ma; my man Block handled everything else," he said, pointing in Block's direction.

"Alright, well let's get out of here son; I got some business to handle. You ready beautiful?"

"Ready when you are," she said as she climbed in the back seat of Amir's car.

"Drop us off at the house ma nigga," Block said as he loaded the remaining bags in the trunk.

Taking his cellphone out his pocket as he got in the car, he placed another unanswered call to Leno's phone. Fed up with not getting an answer, he placed a call to Keisha's phone to find out what was going on once and for all.

"What's good," said Keisha, picking up on the third ring.

"Shit, you tell me, ma nigga, where the hell is Leno? And, why he ain't answering the phone," said Block with irritation present in his voice.

"You made it back from ya trip yet?"

"Yea, I just touched down; what up with the nigga Leno though?"

"Meet me at the unit, I'll be there in thirty minutes," Keisha said, then disconnected the call.

Block removed the phone from his ear and looked at it like it was a foreign object. He couldn't believe that she had hung up on him. He was sure that whatever she had to say couldn't be said over the phone, but it was a common rule of respect to say goodbye to someone before getting off the phone. That's how you let them know that the conversation was over. Nevertheless, he would check her on it when he saw her. He unsuccessfully tried Leno a few more times before giving up completely. He just couldn't understand why he hadn't picked the phone up yet. He looked over at Chasity and asked was she okay. She stated that she was fine and for him to handle his business. She was well aware of how the game went, and she knew that he needed to play catch up after being away for three days. He smiled back at her and continued to look through his phone. He was in the process of texting Flip his head lieutenant when a text came in from Adrian, requesting Block's presence at the unit asap.

"Aye, change of plans son, take me to the unit instead. You can drop beauty off at my spot to pick up her car after you drop me off first," Block said with urgency as he looked up from his phone for a second; he was in the midst of texting Adrian back.

"Everything alright fam?" said Amir.

"Now you know better than that ma nigga," said Block as he looked at him with his lips twisted up and his head tilted to the side.

Amir looked in the rearview mirror at Chasity, who was silently engaged in her phone. From the look on her face, he was sure she wasn't paying them any attention. But, Block had this thing with talking about business around people who weren't associated with the crew.

"Do she know?" Amir asked.

"Yeah she knows, but that's all she need to know, you feel me?"

"I feel you," Amir said as he focused his attention back on the road.

"Hey ma, Amir's gone take you."

"I know, I heard you before when you mentioned it baby; handle ya business future," Chasity said with a wink of an eye, then focused her attention back on her phone.

All Block could do was smile. He was sure that she would feel some type of way about them not riding back to the house together. But, her playing it cool only made him feel better about his decision to wife her. When they pulled up to the gate of the back storage units, he texted Adrian to let him know that he had arrived. He quickly texted back that they were in the chambers. Block put his phone in his pocket as he was getting out the car. He pulled Chasity out for a hug and kiss, then promised to call her later. He looked up to Amir, standing outside the car with his mouth hung open in shock. He had never seen his friend be openly affectionate with any woman before.

"Don't start dude," Block said with a smile. "Matter of fact, mind ya business nigga." He slapped Chasity on the ass before she got back in the car before mouthing the words I'll call you later.

He walked over to the gate and entered the code to gain access to the special storage units where they were awaiting his arrival. He decided to jog the quarter of a mile to the unit they were in, which served as the chambers and his office. When he entered the building, he went straight to the chambers, unsure of what he was walking in to.

"Damn ma nigga, it took you long enough," Leno said as he walked up to him and embraced him in a brotherly hug. "How was your hiatus?"

"It was straight, now what the fuck happened yo?" Block asked as he brushed him off. He was ready to get down to business; he was in no mood for small talk.

"Well, remember the detective I was telling you about?" Well, I had to body the nigga; he was starting to become a real problem for me and I had to make an executive decision," Leno said as he sat down.

"I told you to call me if there was any issues ma nigga. There could've been a better way to handle the situation, instead of killing a fucking cop!" Block yelled out in frustration.

"It had to be done; the nigga had his sights on me for some reason or another, and I couldn't have him fucking up shit, snooping around on a hunch or some shit!" Leno said as stood up and yelled back, equally mad.

"Alright alright, calm down you two!" Keisha yelled as she stepped in between them, placing a hand on both of their chest to separate the two. "Tell him what went down Leonardo, then maybe he'll understand why you did what you did," she said, taking a few steps to the side.

"Alright, so all weekend the nigga been coming by the trap and shit; dude would just sit there for hours on end, not even trying to blend in or nothing. The nigga even followed me to Chelle house! Mannnn, I can't have this nigga knowing where my woman lay her head, fucking with her, trying to get to me and shit. Hell, I don't even know why the nigga on my ass in the first place shit!" an aggravated Leno said, as he paced the floor back and forth while running his hands over his braids.

Block looked on in disbelief as the wheels began to spin in his head, trying to come up with a solution to their newly added problem. When dealing with the streets, everyone knew that it was two people you didn't kill and that's innocent bystanders and cops. Doing one of the two called for added pressure from the mayor and the chief of police, making it damn near impossible for anybody to get money in these streets.

Block stood there in silence for a few more seconds; he took a deep breath before beginning to speak, almost afraid to ask his next question.

"So, what exactly happened leading up to the incident fam? Wait, one of y'all roll a blunt first; I gotta be high to deal with this shit," Block said as he took a seat in the chair next to the torture table.

"Already got you covered ma nigga," Leno said as he pulled a pre rolled blunt from behind his ear, then lit it up. He took a few pulls off of it and passed it over to Block.

"Okay, so like I was saying, we had just left the trap on Ivy St. I was headed to meet Michelle at her house when she got off work. Dude had been following me around for damn near three days and I couldn't take it anymore, so I led the nigga to one of our secluded houses and invited his ass in."

"Which house?" Block asked, interrupting his story. He wanted to know which house to send the cleanup crew to.

"The spot on Briscoe, but me and Adrian already handled that," Leno said, pointing in Adrian's direction.

"Cool! Ma bad, finish what you were saying son," Block said as he took another hit from the blunt.

"But yeah, I took the nigga to the spot on Briscoe. When I got out the car, I figured I would have to do the nigga in right there in his car, but this nigga go out with me. So, I invited him in. I had already put the silencer on my shit when we first pulled up to the spot, so I was good. So boom, we get inside the spot or whatever, right; this nigga start talking bout he knows who I am and all that shit, right. He knows what we do and who my partner is and all that, talking bout he aware of what goes on in the hood and he wanted in, right. So, I laughs at the nigga son; I just couldn't help it cause the shit was funny to me. So boom, he goes on to say that I need to pay him fifty stacks a month for him to turn the other cheek or whatever. But, get this, this nigga goes on to say that we just giving him hush money, and that he'll be damned if he helped a stupid nigger, and I quote 'a stupid nigger survive anymore that society will allow them to'. So, I asked the nigga to elaborate on what he meant, so this mutha fucka goes on to say that he ain't giving us no heads up on twelve, he ain't giving out no information, or nothing. That this was merely hush money and hush money alone. So, I asked him for how long, just for him to humor me right and the stupid fuck says until his son goes off to college or I'm in jail or dead, whichever comes first. Then the nigga said his son was two. Two ma nigga! So while I'm bend over in gut busting laughter, I'm getting ma shit out ma pants right. On my way back up, I put one dead in the center of his chest, then one in the middle of his forehead. Lights out nigga!"

Block sat there with wide eyes and an open mouth for what felt like five minutes but really was only thirty seconds or so. He couldn't believe all this had taken place while he was away on a three-day hiatus. He couldn't help but to think that, if he had only stayed his ass home, maybe things would have turned out different and that maybe this would have never happened. He couldn't understand why things had been going so sour lately. He was extra careful when he made moves, and he was very selective on who he did business with. He was convinced that there was another rat in the building. As long as he been in the game, he'd never been caught up in nothing, and his name had been clean thus far. He'd made sure of that. So, how this nigga claimed to have known them and their operation was mind boggling to him. He wanted to call Captain John to see what information he could get out of him concerning the situation, but that would only bring heat to them, seeing as though they were the ones responsible for his murder. So now, it was just a matter of them covering up all of their tracks to make sure nobody could connect them to the now late Detective Jackowski.

"Wow, okay, so where is the car he drove?" Block asked to no one in particular.

"Adrian already handled that too, son, chill out. I told you we got this," Leno said with satisfaction, then he pulled another pre rolled blunt from behind his ear.

"That's cool and all, but don't all police cars have a GPS in them?"

It was Adrian's turn to speak this time. "Already took care of that; I had my home girl in dispatch erase the tracking info for the entire weekend. The only thing she couldn't erase was him calling in the license plate and ID information from the night Leno got stopped. All that stuff is recorded and backed up on a different system, which basically is connected to the FBI's system. They made it that way to keep local police from tampering with 911 calls and calls made over the radio. But all of that is circumstantial nevertheless, so we're good. Now, I say we dismember the body and remove all body parts that contain DNA information, such as teeth, fingertips, palms of the hands, and feet. All those parts need to be liquefied in acid; the other parts can be burned by regular fire. Let's say we just threw him in the incinerator, right. Well most people don't know that some bones get left behind, like teeth or parts of the skull, just to name a few. But yeah, some of these parts can still be found if you rummage through the ashes, but if we use acid to burn and liquefy the body and do each part that contains identifiable DNA separately, then we lessen the risk of getting caught and someone finding usable DNA to identify him with," Adrian explained.

He was giving them factual knowledge that he'd hope they would understand on the first try because that was a lot of information to grasp and he didn't think that he could make it sound any simpler for them, anything short of drawing pictures, but he

216

would if that's what it'd take for them to understand. He was down for his team and he wanted to make sure they were covered. If he was sloppy, he could take the risk of getting himself implicated in the crime as well and he would never put himself in any harm's way.

"Okay, so what do you need me to do A?" Block asked, still in a daze from all that was being presented to him. He had long finished his blunt and was in need of some exotic shit to help ease his mind.

"Nothing, just let me do what I do best ma nigga, and I promise we'll be straight. I got a guy who supply the acid, so he can get me however much I'd need. You just pay the tab since your money longer than mine and the rest is history," Adrian said as he fixed his imaginary tie.

"Say no more. Keisha, you already know what to do. Holla at me if y'all need me for anything. And let's make this the last time y'all keep me out of the loop, vacation or not, this business comes first ya dig!" Block said as he turned to walk away. "Ayo, let me hit that blunt one time down, and I need you to swing me by the house to get ma whip," he said to Leno.

"Here you go fam," he said, taking another hit then passing it. "Adrian, you straight; you need me to do anything else before I take him to the crib?"

"Nah, I think I'm all set," Adrian said, looking around as if that would help spark his memory. "Yeah, I'm good; y'all go head. I'll hit y'all up if I do."

"Alright, get at me when you done then," Leno said, walking away towards the exit.

As soon as Leno dropped him off at the crib, he went up to roll a few blunts of the motherland and get in the wind. Block made it a point to stop by all his traps to check the scene for his self. He wanted to make sure shit was still running smooth and that they didn't have any more spectators lurking in the cut. He shot his sister a text to let her know he'd made it home safe and one to Chasity, letting her know he enjoyed the time they'd spent, and he would call her later if it hadn't gotten too late.

Block made rounds to every spot he had in rotation. His plan was to put Tank's new spot on Briscoe, but that idea was cancelled due to Leno and one if his trigger happy episodes. He decided to leave it be for now and just split the work up between a few of his other houses, so he wouldn't lose out on any more money.

He received a text from Adrian a few hours later, confirming that situation was finalized. He then decided to call it quits for the day. All the long nights had finally caught up with him and sleep was slowly creeping up on him. He sent Chasity a goodnight text and promised to take her out to lunch one day this week. He still had a few loose ends to tie up with the Loci and Marlon situation, so that was next on his agenda.

Finding Loci, Geechee, and Marlon was proving to be harder than he had initially expected. Months had gone by and he still had yet to run into them. It was as if they disappeared off the face of the earth.

He linked up with Amir and contacted the hit squad since he couldn't locate them on his own. It was imperative that he found them niggas to make them pay for stealing from him. He called the boys, Poseidon and Denim; these dudes were the head of an elite group of contract killers. Whenever he needed a person located or took out without getting his own hands dirty, that was who he called. He didn't want Poseidon to kill them; he just wanted him to find out their whereabouts and let him know.

Things with Chasity had really taken off; they were going into their fifth month of their relationship and the use of the words *I love you* had long been a distant memory. By the end of the first month, they were professing their love for one each other. Since things were starting to get back to normal around the way, Block decided that he would take her to meet his mother and sister early in the day today.

He had a monthly meeting with his lieutenants that was long overdue. The one a few months back had been cancelled, due to the heat of killing detective Jackowski. And now that things were starting to die down a little, with the cops not being out so much, he figured he could allow his men a chance to blow off a little steam. He planned on leaving right after the meeting though; there was no sense in him staying when he had a lady at home. Strippers weren't his type anyway.

Leno and Michelle had become an item as well; hell, they practically lived together. Michelle had a calming effect on Leno whenever she was around. She was like a drug to him; a Xanax to be exact, if you had to choose one. Keisha was coming to terms with her nephew and best friend being together. After seeing the effect that she had on him and how happy he made her, she could only respect their relationship and move forward. She figured there was no sense in losing her only living relative because he was dating her best friend; a woman ten years his senior. She believed that, at the end of the day, you couldn't help who you fell in love with, so who was she to stand in the way of that.

Block was on his way to pick up Chasity from her house to go and meet the two most special women in his life. He was a few streets away from her when he got a call from Leno, telling him to come to the Block asap; there was something that he needed to see.

Pulling up behind Leno's car, he killed the ignition and got out. Walking up to Leno, he gave him some dab and asked him what was up. He noticed the little nigga Pierre standing off to the side, engulfed in his phone. It was something about him that Block didn't like. He couldn't rock with a nigga that played the fence. In his eyes, anybody who was cool with everybody couldn't be trusted, no matter if their intentions were good or not.

"Well, first off ma nigga, let me start by saying that I had no idea that Chasity and Onyx was the same person," Leno stated before Block interrupted him.

"What the fuck you talking about nigga? Who the hell is Onyx? Ma lady name is Chasity, not no fucking Onyx," Block said, slightly aggravated that he rushed over here for this bullshit.

"Son, that's what I'm trying to tell you. You were all secretive with the bitch-,"

"Hold up son, watch ya mouth now; you don't see me out here disrespecting Chelle by calling her a bitch, do you? So, respect mine and watch ya mouth ma nigga," Block said through gritted teeth. Block was big on respect no matter who you were, but he already knew that.

"Ma bad fam, ma bad, but you was all secretive with her identity, not bringing her around and shit. So, how was I suppose to know that you wifed a hoe ma-,"

Before Leno could even finish his sentence, Block had his hand around Leno's throat. He'd already warned him about his mouth, so when he referred to her as a hoe, it sent Block into a frenzy. To him, it was a sign of pure disrespect, best friend or not; respect was a must. Pierre noticed things went left, so he stepped in to separate the two.

"Aye man, let him go B; y'all boys mannn, y'all boys! Cut him loose son!" Pierre yelled out as she tried to remove his hand off of Leno's throat.

Block had the look of death in his eyes; he was trying to process what his best friend was telling him, but he was blinded by love. Twelve years of friendship had no meaning to him at this present point; all he could think about was defending his lady's name.

"Fa real dude, cut him loose; you gone choke ya right hand man out over a hoe! Come on now, where they do that at!"

Block suddenly released Leno from his strong hold. He now had his sights on the fuck nigga in front of him. Leno dropped to his knees, trying to catch his breath. Anybody else would be dead if they tried him like that. But with it being Block, murder never crossed his mind. He could never bring harm to his best friend, even if things got physical.

Block yoked up Pierre and sent a jab to his stomach with his free hand. "Who the fuck is you talking to nigga? Hun? I will dead ya ass right the fuck now; try me if you think I'm bluffing bitch nigga!" Block said with spit dripping from his mouth. Mad was an understatement; Block was on fire.

"Yo, just listen to the little nigga dude, DAMN!" Leno yelled in between breaths. "Put him down son and just listen to him.

Block released him a few seconds later. His chest heaving up and down; his breathing short and quick. "Speak nigga, and it better make fucking sense nigga."

"I was trying to tell you that the nigga Geechee use to fuck with shorty man. The nigga uploaded a video on Facebook of them fucking son. Shorty ass all over the internet dude. Don't believe me see for yourself," Pierre said, pressing play on the video and passing it to him.

"Let me ask you something ma nigga; why you showing me this shit son? What you looking to get out of doing this shit?"

"I ain't looking for nothing ma nigga; shidd, I just don't want you out here looking stupid over no chick that's all. Shid, if it was me, I would want somebody to put me up on game."

"Yeah aight," Block said, giving him the side eye with his lips twisted into a sideways frown.

Against his better judgement, he took a look at it anyway. He really hoped Pierre was wrong and that it wasn't his queen's ass sprawled out all over the internet for the whole world to see. Block drew in a deep breath, once he recognized her in the video. She was making those same love faces that he'd came to love whenever he was balls deep in her pussy.

"How long ago did this fucking happen?" Block asked to no one in particular.

"I don't know son, but like I was trying to tell you before; you put yo mutha fuckin hands on me. I fucked her too."

"You did what!" Block screamed out as he rushed Leno.

"Aye nigga, back the fuck up off of me; that shit was years ago nigga," Leno said, pushing Block away. "That shit was long before y'all met; hell, I didn't even know that she was the same chick you wifed up nigga. I knew her as Onyx, not as no fucking Chasity nigga. I would never sleep wit cho bit-,"

Block looked at him with the side eye, still daring him to disrespect her.

"I mean, I would never sleep with ya girl nigga; come on now, you know me better than that."

Block blew out a long breath before he spoke again, feeling somewhat defeated. "I know nigga this pill is just- it's just a little hard to swallow ya know," he said as he looked Leno directly in the eye.

He then turned his attention back to Pierre, who was still watching the video. "Aye nigga, turn that shit off!"

"Aight nigga, shit, I don't know why you mad at me like I fucked the bitch; shidd, it ain't ma fault you ain't get a vagfax on the bitch before wifeing up a hoe," Pierre said as he laughed at his own joke.

"What the fuck you say to me, nigga? Do you got a death wish or some shit?" Block asked, taking a few steps towards him.

"Shit, I'm just sayin-,"

"You just sayin what nigga?" Block asked, taking out his gun as he rushed up to him and hit him in the head with the butt of his gun.

At this point, Block was filled with pure rage; all he saw was red. All that was replaying in his mind as he repeatedly beat Pierre's face in was him showing him Chasity's ass sprawled out all over the screen. What pissed Block off even more was the stupid smirk Pierre had on his face as Block looked on in horror at his wifey being fucked from behind. Pierre thought Block didn't see his face because he was too engulfed into the video, but he saw him out the side of his eye. Block would have addressed it then, but Leno took his attention away when he said that he had fucked her too. Leno's yelling and

224

tugging on his shit brought Block out of his ass whipping trance. Block was out for Blood and now that he had gotten that, he wanted answers. Block jumped up in a hastily state; his next stop was Chasity's house to get his questions answered.

"Yo, call Adrian and tell him to come clean this shit up. That's niggas dead! And if not, finish him off," Block said as he raced over to his car and peeled out so fast that his tires squealed. He could care less about the few stranglers that stayed around to witness the whole scene unfold. They knew better than to say anything, for fear of the same thing happening to them.

Block made it to Chasity's house in record timing. He turned the corner of her street on two wheels, hitting her mailbox on the way up her driveway. He was so distraught about the situation, he failed to see the two cars that had been following him for miles. He didn't even answer his phone, which had been ringing back to back for some time now. He wanted nothing or no one to stop him from getting his questions answered. Little did he know, it was Poseidon calling to tell him that Loci and Marlon had been tailing him since his last stop. Their job was to find them not kill them, so for now, all he could do was to try and warn Block. Since Block wasn't answering his phone, he would continue to tail them to see exactly what they were up to.

Chasity heard the commotion outside of her house, so she rushed out to see what was going on. Block jumped out the truck, leaving it running with the door open. He raced up the porch steps two at a time, meeting her at the top of the stairs.

"OH MY GOD, baby, you okay? Are you hurt?" Chasity screamed out in reference to all the Blood on his hands and ripped shirt.

"When the fuck was you going tell me that you made a sex tape Onyx?" Block yelled in her face, putting emphasis on the name Onyx.

Chasity stood there with a look of dread in her eyes.

"Yeah, you didn't think I would find out, did you TRICK?"

"Okay Chauncey, ain't no need for the name calling now," Chasity said as she took two steps back to create some space between them.

"Nah, don't be modest now hoe; when the fuck was you going to tell me, hun? What? After we had a baby? Oww, I know; after I married yo thot ass," Block said angrily with spit flying from his mouth.

"Look, that was a long time ago; me and Geechee were in a committed relationship for years when we made that tape OKAY!" she said. Block had never spoken to her that way before, and she didn't like it one bit. She was use to him calling her his future, or his beautiful queen, not him referring to her as a thot. So, she was trying her best to remain calm, since this was not his normal behavior.

"Oh okay, so that was years ago, so that makes it okay hun? So what, you a reformed hoe now?"

"Chauncey, will you please stop talking to me like that? I understand you're upset, and you have every right to be. But I will not stand here and allow you to disrespect me like this!" Chasity said as calmly as could be.

So, that was the boyfriend you broke up with that went to jail for rape?"

"Yes, it was."

"Well, did you know that he was my fucking enemy and that, that was my little sister he raped?" he yelled.

Chasity gasped and covered her mouth with her hand, visibly showing she was unaware and shocked.

"Anddd you slept with my best friend, ma fuckin right hand man! And bitch, don't tell me that you didn't know cause you knew. You knew his name and you've seen his picture on the wall at the house. SO DON'T FUCKING TELL ME SOME BULLSHIT LIKE YOU DIDN'T KNOW!!" Block yelled out at the top of his lungs.

Clearly, they were causing a scene because the neighbors surrounding her house began to come out of theirs.

"Look, let's just go in the house and talk about this Chauncey; you're making a scene."

"I DON'T GIVE A FUC-,"

Suddenly, his tyrant was interrupted by bullets flying directly at them. He grabbed Chasity and tried to pull her down to the floor out of harm's way. But, not before she took one to the shoulder and one to the hip. Block was hit in the right arm, but that didn't stop him from returning fire. As bad as he wanted to help her, he had to knock some of them niggas off before they ended his young life. He proceeded to empty his clip in the direction of the car in front of him. He could have sworn he saw the shooter in the second car aim and shoot at the first car. That's when he realized it was Poseidon and Denim in the second car. After the gunfire ceased from the first car, Poseidon's car sped away. Police sirens could be heard off in the distance, Chasity stayed in a fairly nice neighborhood, so he was sure one of them had called for help. Block dropped his gun on his side as he bent down to tend to her wounds. He took each of his hands and applied as much pressure as he could to keep her from bleeding out.

"Stay with me baby, just stay with me!" he whispered to her softly as he leaned in to kiss her tears away.

"It burns baby; ohhhhh God, it hurts so bad!" Chastity screamed out with tears streaming down her face.

"Shhhh baby, don't speak; save your strength. Where the fuck is the ambulance!" Block hollered out as he looked around.

Everyone had since come back out and formed a circle around the car.

"Man, them mutha fuckas is dead; will somebody please come help me before she be too!" he hollered out to no one in particular.

Just then, an older gentleman came running up the porch steps.

"How bad is it son?" he asked.

"I don't know, but she's hit here and here," Block said, pointing to her wounds in the shoulder and hip.

The salt and pepper haired gentleman removed his shirt and used it to apply pressure to her hip area.

"Now, take off your shirt and cover the one on her shoulder; you need the cloth to help slow down the bleeding. Right now, the blood is just seeping through your fingers.

Block did what he was told and removed his shirt to apply it to her shoulder.

"Son, did you know that you were hit as well?" the man asked.

Block looked over at his arm; realizing that it was just a flesh wound, he focused his attention back on Chasity.

"It's just a flesh wound; I'll live. Come on baby, stay awake; look at me, beauty. Stay awake for me, ma!"

"I'm cold, baby, and sleepy," she said through chattering teeth. Her lips began to quiver, as goosebumps formed all over her arms.

"I'm cold too baby; it is March, you know," he said with a chuckle.

"Here comes the ambulance now," said the gentleman.

"Finally," Block said with a sigh of relief. "Hold on baby, help is here now; just hold on, okay."

Chasity shook her head up and down. The EMT's rushed up the sidewalk with a stretcher and medical bags in tow.

"We'll take it from here guys," the older one said. "Can you tell me how many times she was hit?"

"Just two that I know of," Block said.

"Ma'am, ma'am, can you tell me your name?" the EMT asked.

"Chast- Chasity Freeman," she managed to get out.

"Okay ma'am, we're going to get you to a hospital; just hold on, okay."

"K," was all that she was able to say.

"Okay, Mike, her pulse is getting weak; we gotta go."

"Okay John, we'll lift her up on three, okay. One, two, three. There we go. We'll start an IV in the truck; let's move."

"Is anyone else hurt?" John asked while they assisted the EMT's with carrying her down the steps.

"He's hit," the older man said.

"Mine's is just a flesh wound; I'll be fine. Chasity, baby, I'm right behind you okay."

"Sir, you can ride with us if you like. That way, we can patch you up on the way."

Block agreed, then went to his truck to turn it off and lock it up. He discreetly placed his gun in the glove box and hopped in the ambulance with her. Before they could close the door, a cop walked up and stopped them. He told Block that he was following them to the hospital to get his statement. He nodded his head okay.

As soon as they arrived at the hospital, they rushed Chasity off to the operating room. Block did, indeed, only have a flesh wound, which they patched up on the way over as promised, just as soon as they got Chasity stable enough for the ride.

The officers didn't even give Block a minute to get settled before they started in with the questioning. Block answered the questions as best as any hood nigga could without giving away too much information to the pigs. They ran his name, gave him their business cards, and told him that they'd be in touch and not to leave town. Block couldn't understand what made them madder, him having a valid license to carry or the fact that he came back clean when they ran his name. He reached into his pocket to retrieve his phone and came up empty handed. He'd forgotten that his phone was on the seat of his truck. He walked over to the nurse's station and asked to use their phone. He called Leno up and told him to swing by the hospital and get him, so he could go home and change his clothes. He would stop by her house to get his truck on the way back to the hospital. He wanted to be sure his face was one of the first ones she'd see when she got out of surgery.

On the ride over from the hospital, he explained to Leno how everything went down. When he finished telling the story, Leno was left speechless. Last he heard, Loci and Marlon had gone off the radar; he wasn't aware that they were in town. He was just glad that

Poseidon and Denim was around to back him up. He would make it his business to thank them personally one day for saving his best friend's life. In the meantime, monetary thanks would have to suffice.

"So, are we gonna talk about the shit that happened earlier or what?" asked Leno.

"We can talk about that later dude, for now, I just wanna focus on my girl."

"That's understandable. Well, do you need me to wait while you run up and change your clothes? Or you gone drive another car and get that one later?" Leno asked.

"Nah, I left my phone and gun in that car, so I'ma need you to wait while I take a quick shower and I'll be right out. Give me fifteen minutes' son." Block said as he got out the car.

He quickly ran past security and their questioning stares, up to his penthouse to change clothes. He took a quick wash off and changed into some comfortable clothing. He was in and out in less than fifteen minutes, headed back to Chasity's spot. Her mother's number was saved in his phone; he was dreading the phone call, but he knew it had to be done.

As soon as they arrived at his truck, he hopped out, ready to get back to her side. Leno asked him if he needed him to come along, and he declined. He told him he would call him if he needed him for anything, then made his way back to ECMC hospital. That hospital was more experienced with gunshot victims. On the way over, he said a silent prayer to God, asking him to protect her and keep her alive. He couldn't help but feel responsible; he basically brought the drama to her front door. He wondered how things would have turned out had he been thinking like his usual, rational self. Chasity wouldn't be lying in the hospital fighting for her life right now, that was for sure.

He sat in the truck for a minute to process it all when he arrived at the hospital. He figured he might as well get the phone call over with, no use in dragging it out. Taking a deep breath, he selected her name in his phone and pressed send. She cheerfully picked up on the third ring.

"Hey young man, to what do I owe this pleasure?" Ms. Freeman asked with glee.

"Ma'am," he said, breathing deeply, "Chasity's been shot; we're up here at ECMC. I need you to calmly and quickly to get up here. Do you understand?"

"Shot? When? Where? How? Oh lord, is my baby okay Chauncey? Please tell me that my baby is okay," she said, firing off question after question.

"At this point, Ms. Freeman, I don't know, but-"

"Oh God no, please not my baby, Lord whyyyy!" Ms. Freeman howled out.

"Ms. Freeman? Ms. Freeman?"

"Yes, I'm here. I'm here."

"Ms. Freeman, I need you to calm down, take a deep breath for me, okay!"

"Okay."

"Now, I need for you to calmly and safely get up here as soon as you can, okay. Because if you don't calm down, you could have a wreck and be in the same hospital as your daughter. And that wouldn't do her no good now, would it?" Block said calmly but firmly.

"No, it wouldn't; well, what room is she in?"

"The operating room ma'am."

"Oh lord, I'm on my way now son. Stay with her, stay with my baby okay," she said, rushing to get off the phone.

"I will ma'am; see you in a bit and drive safe," Block said, meaning every word.

"I will, Lord, cover my baby in your blood, in Jesus name I pray. Amen."

"Amen, see you soon," Block said before he disconnected the call. He couldn't take hearing her religious pleas any longer.

Block was in need of a blunt something awful. He was glad he kept an emergency sack in his secret compartment for moments like this. He quickly rolled one up and tapped it a few times before putting it out. He sprayed himself down with cologne, then proceeded to go inside and check on her status.

The ladies at the nurse's station said that she should be out of surgery shortly and, last they heard, she was doing fine. That tad bit of information helped to ease his mind. He grabbed him a soda out of the vending machine, then he got comfortable in the waiting area. He was ready to stay all night if he had to, just to see her face and make sure she was alright.

Thirty minutes into the wait, Ms. Freeman came barging through the doors, screaming where was her baby. He jumped up to intercept her and update her on her status before they called security on the unruly old lady.

"Ms. Freeman, Ms. Freeman!" Block called out. "Come sit down over here, so I can tell you what's going on." First, he updated her on her medical status, then he began to give the PG version of what went down. After listening to his story, she sat still and quite for a few moments.

"Did they catch them?" she asked while staring straight ahead.

"No ma'am, they didn't, they're dead," Block said, placing his head in his hands.

"Did the police kill them?"

Block sat back in his seat; he took a nice long breath before answering her last question. "No ma'am, they didn't."

"Did you kill them?" she asked, leaning into him. Her voice barely above a whisper, as she looked him directly in the eye.

Block looked her in the eye while he remained silent.

She took a deep breath and sat back in her seat while they both remained in deep thought. She placed a hand on his knee and said, "Good," then she looked over at him.

"Excuse me?" Block asked for confirmation purposes; he really didn't need to be excused.

"Good, you did good son," she said with a smile. "God forgive me, but if something happens to my baby, I would kill em dead ma damn self. But my heart hurts a little less knowing you took care of my baby and avenged her attacker. So yes, son, to you I say good job."

Block never confirmed nor denied her assumptions; he did, however, smile to himself knowing her mother was okay with him killing someone, if that was the case, in her daughter's honor, of course.

Their moment was interrupted by an older gentleman in a white coat, calling for the family of Freeman. Ms. Freeman jumped up and announced herself as her mother and him as her boyfriend.

"Well, I'm Dr. Michaels, and Ms. Freeman will be just fine. Thankfully, we were able to stop the bleeding; she was giving us a hard time at first, but we got it under control. We did have to give her a blood transfusion for the amount of blood she loss. Also, the bullet she took to the hip shattered a small portion of her hip, so we had to put a metal plate in its place."

"Oh lord, will my baby be able walk doctor?"

"Yes ma'am, thankfully it only shattered the outer hip. With a bit of physical therapy, she will be able to walk normal in no time. As far as her shoulder goes, she'll need therapy for that too; a few inches over and it could have been fatal. But, thankfully, it wasn't. I've been told by one of my colleagues that she's also a trauma nurse; is that correct?"

"Yes, she is, she works over at Buffalo General," Ms. Freeman said proudly.

"Oh okay, we'll make sure that we take extra special care of her and the baby; we always look out for our own."

"Excuse me sir, did you say baby?" Block asked, speaking up, as he had remained quiet the whole time. Now it was his turn to speak, seeing as though it was his seed she was carrying.

"Yes I did. I'm sorry, were you all unaware of her pregnancy?"

"I'm not even sure she knew, to be honest Dr. I'm sure she would have told me; she tells me everything," Ms. Freeman spoke up.

"Oh okay, well she is right at ten weeks and one day; the baby heart beat is very strong. Of course, we had to give her morphine, something a little stronger for pain, but as soon as she's pain free, we can take her off and put her on regular Tylenol. As far as the baby goes, we think he/or she will be just fine. They were able to survive the initial injury, as well as the major blood loss and surgery. So, I'd say the chance of survival is pretty strong. Of course, we will do all we can to take care of the both of them. Now, unfortunately, only Ms. Freeman can stay; there can't be any overnight visitors in ICU who aren't related to the patient. The nurse will be down to get you both in just a bit but, you sir, will only have a thirty-minute visiting window for the night, but you're welcome to return first thing in the morning at 8am sharp."

"Okay, thank you Dr. Michaels; thank you so very much," Ms. Freeman said with genuine meaning."

"Thank you Doctor," Block said with a handshake.

"You both are most welcome, have a goodnight," Dr. Michaels said before walking away.

"Okay sweetie, now we wait. I can't believe my baby is having a baby," she said with excitement. She reached over and gave Block a loving hug. "Everything's gonna be just fine; we'll just have to nurse her back to health, that's all. Thank you, Jesus; thank you for keeping my only child safe," she said as she lifted her hands towards the ceiling.

"I'm here Ms. Freeman, whatever it takes. I'll be here for her and my baby forever and always," Block said with passion as he gave her a hug.

"I know baby, I know. I think that's her nurse walking in our direction," she said, releasing him from their embrace.

"Family for Freeman?"

"Yes ma'am, we are," she said

"Okay, you can follow me right this way please," said the nurse.

Once in the room, Block couldn't contain his tears. Seeing his queen laid up in that bed with all those tubes hooked up to her made him feel like shit.

"Oh, don't cry hun, she'll be okay; she'll be just fine," the nurse said to him as she wrapped her arms around him in a tight hug. "She's just heavily sedated; she can hear you and she can speak. I don't want her to see or hear you crying, then she'll think something is severely wrong with her, okay. You don't want to upset her and the baby, do you?"

"No," Block said in a childlike voice.

"Ookayy, so just wipe those tears, okay. Alright, she'll be just fine," she said, patting his back. "I'm nurse Jackie; I'll be her nurse during her stay here in the ICU and I'm going to take good care of her, alright."

"Okay, thank you, nurse Jackie; sorry about that," Block said apologetically.

"No hun, you're fine; anybody would be visibly shaken seeing their loved one laid up like this, but I promise it's not as bad as it looks. I'll give you guys some privacy; I'll be back in thirty minutes to get you because only mom can stay," she said before walking out.

He walked over to the other side of the bed and grabbed her hand, the one with the IV in it. He gently kissed her hand as he whispered in her ear how sorry he was. She was still heavily sedated, but she was able to squeeze his hand at the sound of his voice. Her mother was on the other side of her, whispering prayers while stroking her hair. Block stayed there looking at her for fifteen more minutes before he told her mom he would be back first thing in the morning to sit with her. She got up to give him a loving hug and kiss on the cheek before walking him to the door. She said a silent prayer over him as well, as she watched him walk down the hallway.

Block wasn't in the mood just yet to go home, so he decided to stop at Leno's and have that talk. Hell, he actually had some news to tell his old friend. He couldn't believe that just five short months ago, he had just saw her in a club and, now, she was having his baby. Life had a way of changing things around and making you see things differently. Nevertheless, he was happy and ready to be there for her and their baby. Watching her get shot and almost losing her made him see her in a whole new light. He couldn't believe he was ready to walk away from his queen over something she did in her past. Hell, everyone had a chapter in their lives that they didn't speak on, so what made him any different? Block was just more or less mad that he had to find out the way that he did; he would have been more willing to accept it if it came from her mouth, that's all.

Before he knew it, he was pulling up to Leno's house and he hadn't even called; thankfully, his car was there though. He was hoping that Michelle wasn't up there because he really wanted to talk to him about the baby. He preferred to wait until she got out of the hospital and was in the clear before he told anyone else. He turned off the car and sat there going through his phone for a minute before he went inside. He returned Poseidon's phone call first and thanked them for their help; using code, he told them that he would give them an extra fifty grand for having his back. They graciously accepted and stated that they would continue on with the second half of the mission; that was to find Geechee. He shot his sister a text and told her that he would have to reschedule that meeting until further notice. He refused to offer any other explanation at this point but, of course, Charmaine wouldn't let up, so he ignored her remaining text messages. The other missed calls could wait until tomorrow, so he grabbed his half of blunt and went to knock on the door.

"Who the fuck is it?" Leno asked from the other side, already knowing who it was since he had a security camera.

"Open the door nigga; you know it's me!" he yelled from the outside.

"Glad ma bitch wasn't here tonight, or else yo ass would still be standing here nigga." He laughed.

"Yea, whatever, move nigga; it's brick out this bitch."

"Yo ass wasn't saying that shit when I picked you up from the hospital damn near naked," Leno said, laughing at his own joke.

"Whatever dude, you got some bottled water?"

"Bottle water? Nigga, the kind of day you've had, yo ass should be asking for a cup of Hennessey nigga!"

"Yeah, you right; let me get a Corona or something. I'm good on the liquor though," Block said.

"I got you; come on in the living room and have a seat nigga. So, how she doing? I'm assuming she made it; yo ass ain't call me, nigga," Leno said, handing him two beers and a few slices of lemon.

"Yeah, she straight; they had to put a piece of metal in her hip cause it was shattered a little on one side. She's gone need physical therapy for that and her shoulder, but the doctors said her and the baby gone be just fine."

"That's good, wait, hold up; did you just say baby nigga? Did I hear that right?" Leno stood up, actually excited.

"Yeah, ma nigga a baby! What you actually rooting for the hoe now?" Block said in a joking mode but meaning it at the same time.

"Mannn look, I was just mad because Pierre showed me the flick. I knew that shit was gone fuck you up, so I was on some other shit."

"Nigga, you good; I'm over it now," Block said.

"Nah nigga, listen, when me and shorty fucked around, it was years ago on some drunk shit and it only happened one time. If it make you feel any better, I haven't heard nothing bad about shorty for years now. I guess she bossed up and got her shit together. But fa real though, ma bad son; if I knew she was her, I would have been said something to you. And that's on everything, shit, I put that on Trudy nigga," Leno said as he took a sip of his beer before putting it down.

"I know ma nigga, I know. If I can count on any nigga on this earth, I know I can count on you, ya dig!" Block said, putting his fist out for a bump, which Leno graciously accepted.

"Word, but fuck all that shit; we having a baby. Damn, I hope it's a boy!" Leno said, overly excited.

"What you mean we nigga? Me nigga, me, I'm having a baby," he said with a laugh.

"Yea nigga we, yo seed is ma seed nigga. Fuck you mean, I know I'm good fa a godfather position nigga. I know I'm good for that."

"You, already know nigga. What's understood don't even need to be explained. But yo, what happened with that shit from earlier; did Adrian take care of that shit alright?"

"Oh yeah, you already know you straight on that; dude was dead as a doorknob. The nigga face looked like ground beef stuffed inside a cracked coconut yo; the shit was crazy!" Leno said with a laugh. "But yo, check it. Adrian said his boy at the department told him ma name came up a few times in the investigation for Dicktective Jackowski's disappearance," he said, taking another swig from his beer.

"Word, how so?"

"Some shit about tracing his last steps, me getting pulled over, and him pulling ma name up on his computer at the office and shit."

"Damn ma nigga!" Block said with a sigh. "That shit just circumstantial though, right?" Block asked, killing the bottle in what seemed a like one gulp

"Damn, slow down nigga, you know you a light weight," he said with a chuckle. "I think so, but Adrian said I should go away for a while, so me and Chelle gone dip off to Florida or some shit for a few weeks, just till shit die down a bit," he said as he finished the last of his beer.

"That what's up; when y'all leaving though?"

"Tomorrow morning; truth be told, I wanna leave tonight. Shit, get up outta here before they ass come snooping around asking questions and shit, ya know."

"Yeah, I feel you; just call Amir whenever and tell him to gas up the plane. He good at pulling shit together last minute," Block said, taking a swig from his second beer.

"Bet, now that we done got all that shit out the way nigga, what up with the Madden nigga? You feel like getting ya ass whipped real quick or nah?"

"Shit, it's whatever nigga; you ain't said nothing but a word. Hold up, let me spark this blunt first nigga," Block said, taking the blunt from his hoodie pocket.

"Bet, D up nigga cause it's onnn," Leno said, handing him a controller.

"Whatever nigga, don't be crying like no bitch when you lose neither nigga!" Block said with a laugh.

"Fuck that shit nigga, play the game and we'll see," said Leno, snatching the blunt from his hand and taking a hit.

"Yo, let me ask you something real quick ma nigga. Do you think I'm stupid for fucking with shorty? Like, I didn't even think about looking into her past or nothing son; I jus-,"

"You ain't stupid nigga," Leno said, interrupting him. "You was just blinded by a chick with a cute face and a fat ass is all. Shit, it happens to the best of them ma nigga," he said, taking another hit from the blunt.

"Son, it wasn't even that like, it was," Block said with a pause as he focused on his hands in front of him, "it was something about her, ma nigga. Like, when I look at shorty, I see a future. I see ma future, ma nigga; like she had me in a trance or something son. But, whatever it was, from the moment I laid eyes on her, I knew she was the one, you know. Like I can't explain it yo; something in me told me that she was ma queen yo. That she would be ma wife, ma nigga," Block said, looking up at Leno with misty eyes.

"DAMN," Leno said, unknowingly blowing out a breath that he was holding in. "That's some deep shit ma nigga," he said with a pause, "but let me ask you something son; what does it matter now? We all got a past, ma nigga; shit, if we were judged based on our past, then nobody would get redemption, ya feel me. From what I can see ma nigga, shorty makes you happy and, on some real shit dude, that's all I care about. So, fuck whoever got something to say about it. Shit, you already know what I do to niggas who got an issue; shiidd, I give them one, so fuck everybody ma nigga; do what's best for you. Plus, you got a little shorty on the way, so it's a little too late to have buyer's remorse now nigga," Leno said with a hearty laugh.

"Damn son, check you out, tryna sound all smart and shit," Block said with a laugh. "But nah, you right ma nigga, fuck it, it's too late to turn back now. Hell, I couldn't even if I tried; I love her too much," Block said with a smile.

Leno looked at his best friend with a smile; he really was happy for his nigga. He was glad he'd found someone to ignite his fire and bring out the beast in him, all while bringing out the best in him. "Alright, enough of this chick shit ma nigga; D up so you can get this ass whipping nigga," Leno said while laughing.

"Come on nigga, don't be crying after I whip ya ass either nigga," said Block.

They sat around and played a game of Madden 2k15 until a little after midnight. It was a tie; they both had won a game apiece. Block was the first one to call it quits for the night. He wanted to get home in enough time to get some good sleep and be back up to the hospital by eight in the morning.

"Alright ma nigga, I'm out of here like last year. I gotta be up to the hospital by eight tomorrow morning. You be safe and I'll see ya when y'all get back," Block said as he stood up to leave.

"Alright then, ma nigga; I'll try to stop by and see y'all before we head out, if we can," he said, pulling Block in for a brotherly embrace as they slapped hands.

"If you can't, I understand, no harm no foul. But y'all be good ma nigga; see you in a few weeks," he said, walking towards the door.

"Keisha know what's up; she said she'll look after the unit while me and Chelle gone," Leno said, walking behind him, so he could lock the door.

"I figured she would; hell, who else gone do it? But yo, hit me up when y'all touch down, after you get settled in of course," Block said.

"That's a bet, drive safe ma nigga, witcho non drinking ass," he said, laughing.

"Shit, I'm good nigga. I pissed them shits out during half time bitch," Block said with a laugh.

"Yeah alright Mr. I'm good; be easy nigga," Leno said as he closed and locked the door.

Block woke up at seven on the dot, thanks to his alarm. He got up, did a quick set of push-ups and sit-ups, then went in the bathroom to handle his hygiene. He grabbed a fruit salad bowl and a bottle of water on his way out the door. He actually was quite famished; he hadn't had anything to eat since breakfast yesterday morning. With everything that went on, he'd just simply forgot to eat yesterday. He decided he would stop by Tim Horton's and grab him two breakfast bagels to go with his fruit bowl, minus the meat of course. They had yet to upgrade to a pork free menu, so he would settle for an egg and cheese bagel instead.

By the time he made it to her door, it was pushing 8:30am. He stopped down at the gift shop and bought every overly priced flower bouquet they had in there. He was surprised to see her awake and alert when he walked in there. He pushed the cart that he used to carry all the flowers off to the side of the room for now. He was just happy to see his lady with her eyes open.

"Hey beautiful, how you feeling?" he asked with a Kool-Aid smile.

"I'm feeling alright, besides feeling like I've been hit by a Mack truck," she said with a painful chuckle. "Mama, can you give us a minute? Go downstairs and get you a coffee or something okay."

"Okay baby, I'll be right outside the door when you need me," Ms. Freeman said as she got up to leave. "Morning baby," she said to Block.

"Good morning Ms. Freeman."

"Okay, well I'll leave y'all to it," she said, shutting the door behind her.

"So, what exactly happened yesterday? I remember arguing with you and that's about all I remember so far. What were we even arguing about? We never argue, so it had to be something serious."

"None of that matters anymore baby; all that matters is that you and my baby are alive and well. We can talk about that another time, when your feeling up to it. Okay?" Block said sweetly, as he sat on the edge of her bed.

"But, I'm feeling up to it now Chauncey. I wanna know what we were arguing about. Wait, run that back; did you say baby? I'm pregnant? But how? I didn't even know it," Chasity said, rubbing her stomach as if she could feel the baby already.

"Yes baby, we're having a baby; you're currently ten weeks pregnant. I'm so fucking happy right now. I love you so much Chasity; I don't know what I would have done if something happened to you baby," Block said, gently rubbing her face.

"I don't understand; when I woke up this morning, my mom told me that I had been shot twice, but she never said anything about me being pregnant," she said, truly baffled.

"Are you not happy, you don't want to have my baby ma?" Block asked as he stood up real fast, so fast that the movement caused Chasity to slightly cringe in pain. "Damn ma, I'm sorry," he said, gently sitting back down.

"No, it's not that. I just don't know why she wouldn't have mentioned it to me this morning, that's all. But I really want to know why we were arguing Chauncey."

Block dropped his head with a sigh. He slick just wanted to act like the whole thing never happened. He wanted her to focus on getting better for herself and for the baby. But, he knew she wouldn't let up until they talked about it, so he had to get it over with.

"On my way over to your house to get you for brunch, I got a call from Leno. He said he needed to talk to me and that I needed to come over there now. So, when I got there, he went on to tell me that you and him fucked around, but it was years ago when you went by the name Onyx. Then, some nigga named Pierre showed me a video that was posted on Facebook, of you and Geechee having sex."

"Oh my god, on Facebook? How did he even get the video? Oh my god, the whole world saw my naked ass on video. Oh my god, oh my god, OH MY FUCKING GOD!" Chasity began to shout.

"Calm down ma, you gone bust a stitch or upset the baby."

"Fuck the baby, the whole world saw my ass-,"

"So, it's fuck ma baby ma; that's how you feel?" Block asked, visibly hurt.

"No, I didn't mean it like that. I was just... sit back down. Come on, sit back down, continue, I'm sorry," Chasity said apologizing.

"Like I was saying, Geechee put it out there. And the nigga Geechee was the one who raped my sister Charmaine when she was just fifteen. It was his brother Loci and his cousin Marlon who shot at us when we were on the porch arguing. But don't worry about that; them niggas didn't make it. But anyway, we was arguing and I called you names and said some shit I shouldn't have said and, for that ma, I'm sorry. You're my queen and I never should have came at you like that," Block said, putting his head down.

"Hold ya head up baby look at me. You had every right to be mad at me; I knew who Leno was the minute you said his name. But that was in my younger days and it was so long ago, and it was only a one time fling that meant nothing to me. I didn't mention it because it wasn't important, because he wasn't important. You understand? And as far as Geechee goes, I had no idea that it was your little sister that he raped, I honestly didn't. I should have told you everything about my past from jump and, for that, I'm sorry," Chasity said with tears in her eyes. "But you have to understand that, that's not me anymore. I've moved from that and I promise this; I can promise you that, that will never be me again. I honestly have changed, and I put that on ma mutha yo," she said with a chuckle.

"You so corny with yo old ass," Block said as he laughed along with her.

"Yeah, but you love ma old ass though," she said with a smile.

"Always ma, and don't ever forget it either," he said as he gently kissed her on the lips. "Now, can we move pass this now; I've done some things in ma past that I'm not proud of too. So, who am I to judge you, ma?"

"Right, now moving on, thank you for all the beautiful flowers you have ducked off neatly in the corner where I can barely see and smell them."

"You always so extra ma," Block said with a laugh as he gathered up some of the flowers to place all over the room.

"Knock, knock," Ms. freeman said before she entered. Well damn, who died in here?" she said in reference to the dozens of flowers.

"Ma pride," said Block as he looked at Chasity with a wink.

"Awww, that's so sweet. Did you tell her about our baby yet?"

"Well damn, if I didn't yet, you sure did," Block said, laughing.

"Boy, hush yo mouth; Chasity, hunny, we're finally having a baaabbyy," she said, super excited.

"I know ma, but you could have told me earlier," Chasity said with a pout.

"No ma'am, wasn't my place; hell, I didn't get you pregnant. Who better to tell you than the person responsible?"

"I'm gone get both of y'all, watch. Where's my nurse; I'm starving. I'm ready for some real food now. I ain't ate since breakfast yesterday morning."

"Let me go get her for you; she was just walking pass the room going that way," Ms. Freeman said, pointing to the left.

"Okay, well I'll be right here," Chasity said.

"Child hush, where else you gone go?" she said with a wave of her hand.

"Yo moms is a trip; I didn't know she was chill like that. I thought she was one of them holy rollers and shit," Block said.

"Yeah well, it's a lot you don't know about my mother. But we'll save those stories for another day. Come lay with me; you look tired."

"I am baby, I could use a few extra hours of sleep, but I'll be alright."

"No, come on lay down with me and the baby; it's enough room right here on this side. I'm gone take one myself right after I eat," she said, patting that side of the bed.

"Okay but only for a little while; at least until you go to sleep," Block said as he kicked his shoes off and got comfortable.

"Owwww!" Chasity hollered.

"What, what I do?" Block asked, jumping up in a panic.

"Nah, I'm just playing; come on, lay back down," she said while laughing.

"You play too much ma, with yo extra ass."

"Yea, yea, but you love me though," she said, sticking out her tongue.

"Damn right I do, you and my unborn baby," Block said as he rubbed her stomach. He stayed just like that until he drifted off to sleep. Sleep always came easy for Block, especially when he was at peace. At that moment, there in the hospital bed with his futuress and their unborn future, he found the most peace.

Almost a week had passed since Chasity had been in the hospital. Today was finally the day of her release. The doctors said that she and the baby was well enough to go home. They gave her a thirty-day supply of prenatal vitamins, along with her pain medication, and told her to follow up with an OBGYN. Chasity thought it was best if she stayed at her mother's house until she was fully recovered and well enough to be on her own. While she was away in the hospital, someone broke into her house, which was fairly easy since the front door was never locked due to the shooting happening. Block promised her he would replace all that was missing with better stuff, but Chasity wasn't concerned with that; she secretly was ready to move anyway.

Block was due to meet them at her mother's house around three that afternoon, just to give them time to get situated in her new living space. Block was at his house getting a work out in on the treadmill. He couldn't contain his excitement; his babies were being released and he needed a way to burn off some extra energy. Once his set was done, he walked in the kitchen to get him some bottled water and lemon to rehydrate before starting a new set. He heard his phone ringing in the workout room from the kitchen, so he ran to answer it before whoever was on the line hung up.

"Hey Mr. McRae, there's two detectives down here to see you; should I send them up?" Rob from front desk security asked.

"No Rob, don't send them up; tell them I'll be down in a minute," Block said.

"Thank you, sir, will do," Rob said, then disconnected the call.

He went into his room to take a quick rinse off and put on some clothes. As always, Block worked out naked, so he was definitely unexposed at the moment. They probably had more questions about the shooting last week; they did say they would be in touch, so Block thought nothing of it pass that.

Soon as he got off the elevator, he was greeted by the two detectives with a slew of questions.

"How may I help you gentlemen today?" Block asked in his most professional voice. He noticed that it wasn't the same detectives from last week who'd questioned him about the shooting.

"Sir, are you Chauncey McRae?" the first detective asked.

"Yes I am, who's asking?"

"I'm Detective Fisher and this is my partner Detective Wilcox, homicide division. Sir, when was the last time you saw Mr. Leonardo Dupree?" Detective Fisher asked.

"Homicide division? Sometime last week, why do you ask?

"And where about was that?" asked Detective Wilcox.

"At his house. And what is the meaning of this line of questioning, if you don't mind my asking?" Block asked, feeling worried about his friend but frustrated with their evasive behavior at the same time. He wondered what the hell Leno had gotten himself into now.

Last he heard from Leno, him and Michelle was going away for a few weeks, so he was slightly confused. But he had been so focused on Chasity and her situation that he never paid attention to the fact that he hadn't heard from Leno after that day until now.

"Can you remember exactly what day that was?" Detective Fisher asked.

"Will one of you please tell me why the fuck this is concerning my friend?" Block asked, fed up with answering their questions. It was time for them to start answering some of his if they wanted to know anything else from him.

"Sure, we'll answer your questions sir; we'll answer them down at the station right after we get through booking you. Chauncey McRae, you're under arrest for the murder of Leonardo 'Leno' Dupree Jr."

****TO BE CONTINUED****

Thank you for taking the time to read this story.

If you enjoyed it, please leave a rate& Review. Tell A Friend to Tell their friends!!

Word of mouth is an Author's best friend!

I appreciate you more than you will ever know!

- JAE JEWELLZ